What the critics are saying...

"B.O.B.'S FALL is a highly recommended story with more twists and turns than can be revealed in this review, but worth every minute spent reading."~ *Carolyn Crisher Romance Reviews Today*

Rating 5 Blue Ribbon: "Lora Leigh and Veronica Chadwick have done it again with this futuristic tale of erotic romance. The plot is action packed and full of intense emotions. I loved this book and highly recommend it; this one is definitely a keeper." ~ *Angel Brewer Romance Junkies*

5 hearts "Veronica Chadwick and Lora Leigh certainly left me panting for more with this one. The characters are well developed, and extremely likeable from the first. A definite keeper, I highly recommend it." ~ *Julia The Romance Studio*

Law and Disorder: Moving Violations

Gold Star Rating "A hot, sexy, erotic romance, MOVING VIOLATIONS has everything needed to make it an intriguing story that's hard to put down." ~ *Reva Moore Just Erotic Romance Reviews*

The Warlord's Gift

4 1/2 Stars "This is a splendid start to the The Kingdom's Redemption series. Linea and Draven are vivid, sensual characters and the world is aptly described. The secondary characters are fully drawn and otherworldly creatures add atmospheric touches."~ *Page Traynor Romantic Times Book Club Magazine*

LORA LEIGH
VERONICA CHADWICK

B.O.B.'S FALL

ELLORA'S CAVE
ROMANTICA PUBLISHING

B.O.B.'S FALL
An Ellora's Cave Publication, April 2005

Ellora's Cave Publishing, Inc.
1337 Commerce Drive, Suite #13
Stow, Ohio 44224

ISBN #1419951807

Other available formats: ISBN MS Reader (LIT), Adobe (PDF), Rocketbook (RB), Mobipocket (PRC) & HTML

Edited by: *Sue-Ellen Gower*
Cover art by: *Syneca*

Warning:

The following material contains graphic sexual content meant for mature readers. *B.O.B.'s Fall* has been rated *E-rotic* by a minimum of three independent reviewers.

Ellora's Cave Publishing offers three levels of Romantica™ reading entertainment: S (S-ensuous), E (E-rotic), and X (X-treme).

S-e*nsuous* love scenes are explicit and leave nothing to the imagination.

E-*rotic* love scenes are explicit, leave nothing to the imagination, and are high in volume per the overall word count. In addition, some E-rated titles might contain fantasy material that some readers find objectionable, such as bondage, submission, same sex encounters, forced seductions, etc. E-rated titles are the most graphic titles we carry; it is common, for instance, for an author to use words such as "fucking", "cock", "pussy", etc., within their work of literature.

X-*treme* titles differ from E-rated titles only in plot premise and storyline execution. Unlike E-rated titles, stories designated with the letter X tend to contain controversial subject matter not for the faint of heart.

B.O.B.'s Fall

Gaelic Glossary

Tha thu brèagha - You are beautiful

Mo milis rós - My sweet rose

Mo' Dia - My God

Mo cridhe - My heart

Ghrá mo cridhe - Love of my heart

Prologue
December 2375

"Mac" MacDougal knew he was dying. He could feel the blood pumping from his body, rich and hot, the elixir of life spilling from his veins despite the desperate attempts of his bodyguards to staunch the flow. He was bleeding out like a gutted pig and there wasn't a damned thing anyone could do to stop it.

"Hurry, goddammit it. We're only a mile from the lab. I've radioed ahead, we have only one chance here, so let's hurry."

He heard his sister, Amareth screaming at the guards and wanted to smile at the cold, hard determination in her voice. If sheer stubbornness alone could have pushed the blood back into his body and repaired the damage inside it, then she would have accomplished it.

She was as strong and as determined as he raised her to be, but for a moment, just for a moment, he regretted the necessity of the lessons he had been forced to teach her, the dreams he knew she had lost in the process. Once, the fiery sister he loved so dearly had been full of dreams and fairytales. Now, she was pragmatic, logical and cool as she ran his security department with an iron will. And now, so close to death, Mac realized he missed the little girl who swore she once saw fairies.

Hell, in one blinding, shocked second, he realized he missed himself. He wasn't the man he had been either. He had shut himself off, had broken ties to any commitments or affections except those of his immediate family. His life had centered around his vast holdings and the routing of the rebels who still fought against planetary order and democracy. Their deaths had fueled him for over a decade, leaving room for little else.

He was being moved. Pain seared his insides with such agony that he lost his breath. Lost it and nearly didn't regain it. He gasped, hearing the betraying wheeze of his lungs filling with blood, his body weakening, his heart attempting to slow.

He was only distantly aware of the ride to the nearby lab he had been attempting to get to. The security he had set up there had somehow been compromised, despite his best-laid plans.

That was the reason he had been rushing for the labs. Among other things, the MacDougal labs worked on the most advanced, most high-tech weapons in the world. Somehow information had leaked from those labs and the design schematics for one of their new weapons had ended up in the hands of a competitor, a known rebel sympathizer. He was going to kill the bloody bastard responsible, if he didn't die first.

This was the reason why he had raised Amareth to be so strong, to be cool and determined in the face of danger. They had been betrayed, and obviously by someone they trusted.

"Get him in there." Amareth's voice pierced his consciousness again. Strident and sharp, she motivated his men as he was certain no one else could.

"We aren't prepared for this. We have only one unit available," an unfamiliar male voice was arguing abrasively. "This won't work. There's no way it will work."

Mac tried to concentrate, to center himself on the fight he could sense raging around him.

"It's our only chance. Do you have any better fucking ideas?" Amareth was screaming.

"No." Breathless, frightened, the male responded. "But Ms. MacDougal, it wasn't designed for this."

He heard a squeak, a gasp.

"Listen to me, you little mouse. If my brother dies you'll follow him within seconds. Remember that." Amareth's voice was low, dangerous, just as he had taught her. Damn, she was becoming a force to be reckoned with. "I know what we designed it for, I know how it works and I know we have a chance, and slight though it is, it's better than watching him die."

The pain was becoming more distant now. Hollow, as though he were somehow disconnected from it. And he was tired. So amazingly weary. He hadn't realized in all these long years how tired he was becoming.

No! He would not die. He had too much work to do, too much to accomplish. Dammit, he still hadn't cleared his schedule enough to hunt up that irritating novelist who had been filling his sister's head with all those ideas of romance and "happily ever afters" that didn't exist.

He might regret the necessity of the strength he had encouraged within her, but his pride in it ran deep. If he did die, Amareth would move on, she would never fall to the predators awaiting her or give in to the lies most women were so hungry to believe in this day and age.

Love wasn't the fairytale Ms. Elyiana Richards wrote it to be. It wasn't soft, it wasn't gentle, it wasn't a hero who strived for happily ever after. It was cold, relentless, destructive. It was a word used to trip and deceive and use the gentle hearts that soon grew hard with weariness and broken promises. He couldn't let Amareth fall to the lies. He had to live long enough, fight hard enough to make certain Ms. Richards realized the fool she was.

But for a moment, just a moment, the image of the Australian spitfire flashed through his mind as she had been during their last vid-phone conversation. Irate, her violet eyes flashing, her lush mouth pouting, she had made him so damned hard, so damned fast, that it had almost taken his breath. She was an innocent, despite the erotic novels she wrote, despite the fact that she had stood up to him with a female fury that made his guts ache to possess her. She was incredibly fresh, fiery, and she made him want things, regret things he had no business thinking about.

He forced himself to pay attention. Tried to grit his teeth, tighten his muscles. He put every ounce of his force into paying attention, to following the little impulses building in his brain…

Amareth stood aside, watching with narrowed eyes as the doctors and scientists that were gathered in the MacDougal labs worked around her brother. The wounds were horrific. One on his chest, abdomen, his thigh was shattered and he had lost an incredible amount of blood. Most of it stained her leather pants and what was left of her black shirt. She had used most of the cloth to attempt to staunch the flow of blood.

Thank God they were close enough to the lab and its medical facilities to give him a chance. That was all he needed. A chance. Mac was strong and stubborn. He wouldn't go away and leave her alone without a fight and she would make damned certain he had every chance to survive.

She watched as the android unit was whisked from another room, biting her lip as she remembered her own smug satisfaction at the design of the sex droid. It was a close resemblance of the MacDougal during his younger, wilder days. Six five with long flowing red hair and piercing light green eyes.

Though the unit retained Mac's strong, incredibly determined features, they had been softened, the scar on his cheek was absent, as was the evidence of a once broken nose. The android didn't have the savagery of expression Mac did, the evidence of a life led through the horrors of guerilla rebels and the loss of loved ones.

Now, the droid would hopefully house the incredible power of her brother's mind and give them a chance to find out who had made the strike against him. Whoever betrayed Mac had been close to him, a vital part of his information network or they would have never known where and when to strike. The visit to the labs had been in secrecy, with only a few people aware of his destination.

The information he had relayed to her as she led the bodyguards to his location indicated that the attackers had known exactly where to find Mac and how to attack.

Dammit, Amareth, we have a mole. Find that fucking mole if I don't survive this…

Mac had obviously come to the same conclusion. Despite all their safeguards, someone had betrayed them.

"You'll find him yourself, Mac," she whispered as he was placed into the specially designed life support unit, electrodes attached to his head and leading to the droid beside him. They couldn't afford to be without The MacDougal, not for a day. Not now.

"Clear…" The head scientist called for an evacuation of the area around the stasis unit. He glanced at her nervously. "What if this doesn't work?"

She smiled. A cold hard curve of her lips that Mac had taught her.

"Then you and everyone in this lab die. Period. I won't tolerate failure, doctor. I can't afford to."

They knew she would do it. Her reputation as The MacDougal's head of personal security hadn't come without a cost. She was willing to back up every promise, every threat she made. She might not like it, she might regret the decisions she made with every fiber of her being, but she would carry it out.

He blanched, but she noticed he took extra care as he began to prepare for the transference of information from her brother's brain to the mechanical body on the gurney beside him.

The droid had been designed just for this, to accept and process the memories, emotions and sensations, as well as the retrieval of vital data from the human mind.

The discovery and isolation of the brain's electrical impulses and the paths they used for human responses, movements and sensation had spurred the creation of the sexual droid and its intricate computerized brain. They had experimented with the information transferal more than a dozen times and, in each case, it had been an unqualified success. She could only pray it would succeed this time as well.

Amareth had never imagined the droid would be needed for this, though.

She watched as the electrodes between her brother's head and the computerized brain of the droid's began to light up in response to the commands being sent between the two. The brain was a computer, a living, constantly evolving work of art that had amazed scientists and doctors for centuries. The discovery of a living, central databank deep within the mass of tissue had been a breakthrough unlike any other. It had allowed the scientific field to create a similar "brain" for the droids that to this point were automated and incapable of processing logical thought without the proper commands.

The original droids had been created for security purposes to protect against attacks made by the rebels in many of the more populated areas of the world. Since then, the models had advanced. Several other companies had created lesser versions of the sex droid, but Amareth had seen a potential there that had been as yet unrealized. If she could make the droid "real" enough, then sales of the models could become astronomical.

It hadn't been created to use in these circumstances, though. Its electronic brain was made to store only the knowledge in the physical functions of the brain. The sense of taste, smell, the ability to appear "real" despite their cybernetics. They were now going to have to attempt a much larger upload.

She fought back her worry, her concern that the new advanced model the MacDougal's company, Cyber-Tronics, had put together, was capable of holding the information stored in Mac's incredible mind. He was, quite honestly, a genius. His mind was lightning fast on its own, his ability to process thought and intuition never failed to amaze her.

"Readings are positive... We have information transference. Begin slowing down life functions, attach all sensors and neural responders; let's get him into stasis until we can get the surgeons and life response experts here..." The scientists worked steadily to prepare Mac's blood-soaked body for the partial shutdown.

Vital organs had to be stilled, repaired and allowed to heal. Blood had to be replaced and the physical body encouraged to allow the healing of its wounds. Placing Mac so deep into the coma-like sleep required was incredibly dangerous. The human will fought the shutdown of vital organs unconsciously, creating a battle that too often ended in the loss of life.

"Get ready to close the wounds and begin blood transfusions," one of the doctors called out to the medical team. "We have a priority alert out to Med-Tech. Surgeons will be heading here within hours. They are estimating a twelve-hour response time on the team."

"They have ten," Amarath snapped. The stasis unit wasn't built to sustain life past twelve hours.

"Impossible..."

"I can break you, doctor, with my bare hands," she growled, deepening her Scots burr, attempting to emulate the brother she had idolized all her life. "Don't make me do that."

The doctor swallowed tightly, a grimace crossing his haggard face as he ran his hand over his balding head.

"Nurse, contact Med-Tech. We have ten hours, stat." He was scared, nervous enough to make certain her demands were followed to the letter.

Of course, the powerful little lazer rifle she carried, and the power she carried while Mac was down didn't hurt anything.

"Jaime, shut down this facility until they arrive," she snapped. "Take four men with you and call in Tael. He'll be awaiting information. Tell him to get his arse up here."

Jaime was watching the proceedings almost fearfully. Mac was his brother, too, though he was still too young to understand the significance of being The MacDougal's brother. He nodded quickly though, motioning to his most trusted men and heading out of the room.

He resembled Mac much too closely. His body was still too tall to truly look good with his youth, his brilliant red hair and green eyes stood out too clearly at this point, but even with the gangly, puppy dog phase he still seemed to be going through, he was just as smart, just as well-trained as Mac had taught him to be. She feared though, that in time, much of the enthusiasm and zest for fun that she saw in Jaime's eyes would dim with the harsh realities of life.

"Zach, guard that door," she snapped as the information transference ended and the electrodes were disconnected between her brother and the droid.

"We have a twelve hour downtime for defrag in the droid, no less," the scientist informed.

"I am aware of that, doctor," she sliced him a cold, hard glance. "I've been in on every stage of development if you haven't forgotten. The defrag will take twelve hours, six minutes and forty three seconds if I'm not mistaken." She lifted a brow sardonically, staying hard, strong, as she knew Mac would expect her to do.

She watched as a nurse wheeled the droid to the next room, frowning at the sudden lurching of her stomach, the heavy beat of her own heart. She could feel her skin prickling in warning but couldn't make sense of the response.

"Tael is on his way, Amareth," Jaime stepped quickly back inside the room. "He's called in three units. They're arriving by jet glider within the hour. We have complete lockdown on the facility with automated security running."

Amareth breathed in deeply. She wasn't falling apart. Everything would be okay. Mac would survive this. She would make certain of it. She stared back at the doctors working over her brother's body, repairing the incredible wounds to his flesh as blood was replaced as quickly as possible.

Life support electrodes covered every vital portion of his body, working to keep his heart, lungs and organs functioning until the professionals could repair the damage. There was time. She knew there was. If Mac was dead, she would know it. She knew she would. But she could feel him living, she could *feel* his strength close to her. As long as she had that, she could go on.

Finally, more than an hour later, the doctors called for the stasis seal. Amareth stepped close to his body, her hand reaching out to smooth back a lock of dark auburn hair from his brow before the unit closed.

The minute she touched his skin she stilled. Fear slammed into her, rocking her to her soul. Mac wasn't there. She trembled, forcing back her panic, stilling the scream building in her throat. She *knew* he was alive, but he wasn't here. Not in his body.

"Oh my God..." she whispered as a freezing chill chased over her body. "Oh my God, what did we do...?"

Suddenly the room filled with the raucous sounds of the internal alarms and the warning of a security breech.

"We have exit, south bank. Warning, we have exit, south bank, jet glider in flight..."

She turned, running for the next room, for the droid placed there more than an hour ago. She threw the door open, knowing what she would see before she entered the room, knowing in that heartbeat, that Mac would kill her for sure when he realized what had happened.

It was gone. The defrag was incomplete, information would be a jumbled mass inside the droid's electronic brain...Mac's brain. Her brother was now helpless...

Chapter One

He would be damned if he would allow himself to be as helpless as he felt.

He awoke, laid out on the gurney like a sacrificial lamb to the slaughter, feeling just as vulnerable, just as weak as the hapless animals that gave their blood to ancient altars. He refused to allow it.

The imperative need to escape, to distance himself was uppermost. He could hear the soldiers moving through the hallways, shouted orders and blasphemous curses rang through the din of chaos as a strident, cold female voice echoed from the next room.

He couldn't remember why he was there, but he remembered pain and blood and the knowledge that he was going to die unless he escaped. Escape became most important.

It was a simple matter to move through the darkened lab. He knew this room, he didn't know why, or how, but the general layout was familiar to him. He slid the khaki overalls from a closet, as well as a pair of ankle boots and dressed quickly. There were no weapons, and he knew he desperately needed a weapon.

"Tael's inbound. Tael's inbound." The sound of a young man's voice echoed in the other room.

"Get his arse down here," the female called out, her tone furious. "We need all the help we can get right now."

His eyes narrowed as he heard the steady drone of powerful jet gliders moving in overhead. Quick, efficient, and capable of taking him wherever he needed to go. The jet gliders were his best hope.

He brushed back his long hair with a grimace of distaste. Hadn't he cut the long, dark red strands ages ago? What the hell were they doing aggravating him now?

There was no time to tie them back. He snarled silently as the doors to the next room slammed and the corridor suddenly became eerily quite. Cracking the door he checked quickly. Seeing the brightly lit, empty hall he made his decision and moved quickly from the room.

He kept his head high, his expression closed and enigmatic. He wouldn't be stopped if he kept his demeanor low-key. He might not be fully aware of who he was yet, or what had happened, but a few things were filtering through.

His name was Mac. His hair was too fucking long and he had to find Elyiana. Those thoughts were like a drumbeat inside his brain, zipping around inside his head and pushing him to hurry. He would be too late if he didn't hurry.

Was she in danger? He saw her smile, the color of her violet eyes, heard her voice, angry but musical, the soft accent drowning his senses. But that was all he could remember. All he knew for certain.

Ahead, metal doors banged as a man's furious voice cut through the sudden din.

"Goddammit, find him. Go ahead and kill the bastard because if you don't, Amareth is going to de-bone him before we get any information out of him anyway."

Mac flattened himself inside the doorway of what appeared to be a darkened communal hall. His teeth clenched as he fought the tingling in his head, like the drone of angry wasps buzzing within his ears. What the hell had they done to him? He shouldn't feel this way, dammit, he shouldn't even be alive.

The sense of that was stronger than anything else inside his suddenly fuzzy, foggy brain. He shouldn't even be alive.

The group passed him quickly, heading in the direction Mac had come from. They had to be the ones who had flown into the area in the jet gliders. Men as hardened as the one leading the group sounded had to be military, or at least ex-military. Those men didn't fly sloppy gliders. They flew the best.

A tight smile crossed his lips at that knowledge. His head was as scrambled as eggs in the morning, but some things were universal. Well-trained men had well-made toys. It was as simple as that.

He waited until the corridor was clear once again before moving from the darkened room and striding confidently through the corridor. It would get trickier from here on out. Just ahead were the glider bay access doors. He could get to the bay, but there was no way he could take off without being noticed. And without clearance, he would have company in ten seconds flat.

He stepped through the metal doors, staring intently at the sleek, two-seater gliders. The black, eagle design of the crafts were a testament of beauty, skill and technology. They were the fastest, the lightest, the most maneuverable. They were also equipped with GPS ghosting. He could block the automated signal for hours while in the air, indefinitely on ground.

He moved quickly for the lead bird. It was mounted with precision lazers, a dark sunshield and gleamed with a shine that had been applied by a loving hand. The pilot of this little beauty would regret its loss more than most, but only because it was the best of the best.

Checking quickly for spying eyes, he deftly mounted the high step and swung himself into the glider. The seat cushioned even his large body as though it had been made for him alone.

"Welcome, Mac, where shall we fly today?" The onboard computer asked the question in well-modulated, faintly accented tones.

For a moment, surprise registered in his system. How had the computer known him? Few Gliders had personalized computers for the simple fact that it made them much harder to repossess should their owners fail to complete payments or in the case of their deaths.

The information was there in his head. Somewhere. Mac assured himself that he would remember it in time. Until then, his most pressing need was escape.

"Destination coordinates delayed. Close shield and prepare for manual flight. Disengage all GPS."

Mac gave the orders crisply as he gripped the manual flight stick and pressed the appropriate switches for manual control.

"You have five seconds before bay doors retract. Alarms have been sounded, Mac. Do you wish to disengage?"

He ignored the computer's voice, maneuvered the stick toward himself as the craft lifted from the bay floor, hovered, then with a quick forward shift of the flight stick, the black glider shot from the bay into the black velvet night.

"Computer, GPS ghost, all flight recorders on board only, block all transmissions and prepare for coordinates," he ordered coldly, ignoring the thickening of the brogue that began to fill his voice.

Damn, it made itself known at the most inconvenient moments. The thick accent was one he would cover if possible. But it slipped out during high stress.

He shook his head as a growl rumbled in his throat. The heavy drone was echoing in his head again as he fought for answers, making it difficult at best to pull free memories he knew he had to have right now.

What the hell had happened to him? He had been hurt, but evidently not as severely as he thought. The imperative demand echoing in his head was all he could truly make sense of. Find Elyiana. He had to find her, though the thought brought equal spurts of lust and fury. He couldn't remember why he had to find her. Couldn't remember what he wanted with her.

She would have to have the answers.

"GPS is now in ghost mode, flight recorders are onboard only, all transmissions are blocked and waiting coordinates," the computer reported mechanically.

Mac stared at the onboard map for a second before quickly inputting the data needed rather than speaking it aloud. It was possible to tap into onboard recording if one knew what they were doing. They couldn't track him, but they might hear him.

"Coordinates received." The eagle banked sharply before gathering speed and hurtling towards its destination.

The estimated time of arrival flashed across the computers onboard screen as ordered when coordinates were given. Two hours. He leaned his head back against the seat, closed his eyes and fought the need to sleep. Each time he felt himself drifting that damned drone in his head brought him abruptly awake. It wasn't normal. There was something about the sound that filled him with dread, made him aware of the precariousness of his position at the moment. He couldn't remember what the position was, but he knew instinctively there was nothing good about it.

He knew where Elyiana was, and how to get there, but he had to figure out why it was so important. It would take more than two hours to put that together, he knew.

Chapter Two

The story was flowing now, right into another very hot sex scene. Elyiana leaned forward and cranked up the volume on her stereo. "One of These Nights" by The Eagles, an ancient band from the twentieth century, filled the house. Music almost always set the mood, inspired her writing, especially music from the old world. It was music that had been all but forgotten; the discs were scarce and extremely valuable. Adding to her collection had been the first thing Elyiana had used some of her royalties for. She cherished every single disc she owned.

With a sigh, Elyiana shifted to a more comfortable position in her desk chair and closed her eyes, letting the scene play out in her mind. Really, she shouldn't use The MacDougal's likeness as the hero in her new novel. Not so soon after she so blatantly used him in *The Laird's Downfall*. But besides the fact that the sales for *The Laird's Downfall* had been higher than any of her other novels, he was an inspiring figure.

Physically he was beautifully sculpted, but it was what he hid inside that intrigued her. Consistently closed off, he appeared dogmatic and unemotional. Some considered him that much more appealing for his aloofness. Elyiana found him infuriatingly self-important and enjoyed making him, through her hero, lose his iron-fisted control as he slowly lost his heart to the heroine. It was merely icing on the cake that it so thoroughly pissed

The MacDougal off when he realized it was him she used in her erotic novels. Clever man.

Absently she wondered if The MacDougal would be anything like the way she depicted him in bed or would take his own pleasure, leaving the woman wanting. More than likely, she thought. He'd probably expect said woman to orgasm at the very thought of being beneath him. No man was that cold, surely, she thought shaking her head.

She smiled to herself remembering his last call. Hell, he should feel honored that she didn't characterize his personality as perfectly as she had his likeness. *"You should read it again MacDougal," she'd told him. "Learn from it. Perhaps then you'll find how to actually please those poor women who've been tolerating your adolescent fumbling for the coveted privilege of having the omnipotent MacDougal in their bed."*

He had been irate, but then so had she. A woman who wasted her time filling her head full of fantasy and romance was weak and utterly useless, huh? Remembering it now made her blood boil. He'd accused her of not only setting herself up as an impressionable nitwit and a victim; he said she did the same to every female who read her "idealized foolishness".

At the time she'd been furious at his archaic male notions of sex and propriety. Had he even read her books? The heroines were always strong women. Women who overcame and conquered. He had shocked her to her core when he said, *"…sex is merely a physical release, a chemical reaction, nothing more."* But now she couldn't help grin at the way he'd growled, threatening her. Perhaps he could deny it to himself, but he was hot-blooded. Damn hot, and it was more than a little intriguing to discover there was passion behind that stone wall he had built up around him.

The man did look good, she thought, as she shifted her focus back to her scene. *The warlord, his big body lying between her thighs, his long dark auburn hair trailing over her feverish skin as he moved down her body. His hands, large and calloused, cupped her breasts, rasping over her beading nipples before his mouth covered them. Hungrily he'd draw on them, his teeth scraping, his tongue laving the aching peaks.*

Watching her, his sea-green eyes darkening with lust. Straight white teeth nipped at her stomach, her navel, his tongue soothing the bite. "Mmm yeah, that's good," Elyiana whispered to herself as she leaned forward and began typing.

Her own body grew warm, the muscled walls of her sheath tightening with a building ache. She bit her bottom lip as the words flowed onto the screen as her fingers flew across the keyboard. Arousal pulsed through her with every teasing bite, every lick her hero bestowed upon his woman's quivering body.

Elyiana's head fell back on a moan and she lifted her shirt to cup her own breast. As much as she hated to acknowledge it, there was something about The MacDougal that reached out to her. On some level she connected with him. Just thinking about him at times made her body flush with heat, moisture gather and saturate the swelling folds of her pussy. Smoothing a hand down her stomach, she unsnapped her shorts and let her fingers comb through the soft curls. A soft moan escaped her lips as her fingers slid through the silky slickness.

Already her clit was a tight bud throbbing against her fingertip. Tilting her chair back, she spread her legs wider as she plunged two fingers inside her tightening sheath.

The scene continued to play out in her mind as she imagined The MacDougal touching her, kissing her. His fingers, slick with her arousal, skimming over her clit, thrusting inside her to massage just the right spot. Or his mouth, those full, firm lips closing over her hardening clit instead of pressed together in anger. She rotated her hips against her hand as she squeezed her taut nipple with the other.

In her mind, she watched him rise above her, his eyes narrowing as the head of his cock probed at her entrance. So good, the weight of him against her would feel so good, his lips hot against her skin, his thick cock invading, stretching her open, forcing her to take all of him. It didn't take long for her to peak. A throaty groan vibrated low in her throat and she arched her back as the orgasm crested, gripping her entire body as it tore through her. Slowly she circled her clit with her finger as the pleasure continued to pulse through her. It built again, sharper this time, with the slightest edge of pain. Trembling, she rode it out 'til another orgasm hit her, harder this time and she cried out, struggling for breath.

She closed her eyes and lay her head back for a moment allowing her blood pressure to lower, her breathing to regulate as the tingling aftershocks softly rippled through her. It was entirely possible that she was letting her fantasies get away with her. The MacDougal could very well have a short little pencil-dick. It wasn't like it mattered whether he did or didn't. It was her fantasy, her story. The power lay in her hands and she could do with her characters whatever she deemed appropriate. Unlike his entourage, she wouldn't shake with fear and scurry to do his bidding, or stop doing something she loved just because he didn't like it.

There was an edge of violence about The MacDougal, a promise in those cool light green eyes that there would be no tenderness, no love, no mercy. Everything she opposed and yet she'd found it incredibly arousing. There hadn't been that many lovers in her past and they had all been gentle and giving. It wasn't that she minded that, on the contrary. What woman didn't love to feel cherished and worshiped?

But at the same time, what woman didn't want to be taken? Ravished. With the slightest bite of pain, not enough to really hurt, just enough to intensify, sharpen, take the pleasure a step up.

A wicked idea came to her and she leaned forward to get back to work. Yeah, this heroine liked things a little rough around the edges, and the hero was going to be very pleased to accommodate her needs. She'd have to go back through the story and do some layering, which might put her a little behind deadline. Aah, the hell with it. It would be worth it.

The scene ended up being nearly two and a half chapters long. She sincerely hoped the readers would love it. The MacDougal would be livid. With a mischievous smile she saved her work and stood to stretch. Too much pent-up energy, she thought. A swim would be a perfect break. It would give her time to think about the changes she was going to make to her story. She shut the computer down and began stripping off her clothing on her way to the bedroom. With her clothes unceremoniously dumped in her hamper, she grabbed the coconut oil and a towel and headed out.

The brisk walk to the beach allowed Elyiana to work up a good sweat and helped loosen the muscles that had stiffened from sitting at her desk for so long. She ran across the hot sand, dropping her towel along the way. The waves were great for surfing. Any other time she'd have brought her board. But today she was feeling reflective and anxious to finish her book and needed time to think through how she would revise it.

Warm water enveloped her as she waded in, diving under the waves, letting them carry her out 'til she could barely keep her footing before she began swimming back to shore. She couldn't help smiling as she walked back to where she'd dropped her towel, spread it out and sat down. God, she loved it here. The sand, the sea—all of it was glorious.

She wondered if the MacDougal had ever been out of the office. A vision of his face appeared in her mind as she laid back and let the sun bathe her. His hair, so dark it was almost black shot with strands of copper and auburn, was close cut and never out of place. Those incredibly sexy eyes were determined, his full lips pressed together in a stern expression. Always serious. She tried to imagine him laughing, or at least smiling and it wasn't easy. But somehow imagining him hot and hungry was.

Those beautiful crystal green eyes of his had darkened, smoldering when he'd called her to bitch her out and threaten to stop publishing her. They narrowed in anger, in lust. It was hard to tell which. Either one, it got her wet, made her want to touch him, want him to touch her. Even now, her body responded to merely thinking of him. Writing intense sex scenes featuring The MacDougal drove her crazy. Imagining him fucking her in every conceivable position. Wide palms molding her breasts, long strong fingers gently squeezing her nipples as he wildly thrust deep inside her. Pushing her to her limit. Making her scream for more, even more.

Frowning in frustration, she rubbed her oiled hands over the peaks of her breasts and hissed at the flare of sensation that radiated through her. The coconut oil had warmed in the hot sun and felt delicious gliding over her skin. Letting it dribble over her stomach and lower, through her thatch of curls. With a sigh, she set the bottle aside and slid her hands over her middle.

Oily fingers slipped lower to delve inside the lips of her pussy. Her fingers slowly glided over her clit. It felt so hot, so slippery. The heat building inside her matched the sun's blazing caress. It didn't take long for the lazy orgasm to possess her. She whimpered as it poured over her long and fluid.

Lying there, she drifted on the fading waves of her climax. As nice as it was, it left her feeling empty. Fantasy unfulfilled could be a vicious bitch, she thought to herself. With a groan, she sat up and crossed her legs, looking out over the ocean, the breaking waves that rolled up on the shore, then away. She was so very content with her world, the beauty of this wild land and all that she had accomplished. Was contentment enough? she'd often asked herself. And each time the answer came back to her. *All in due time, Elyiana. All in due time.* She stood and brushed the sand from her body as best she could. Heading back, she followed the winding path to her home. She took her time enjoying her walk, the lush beauty of the foliage surrounding her home, the fragrant blue haze of the eucalypts evaporating in the heat, the brilliance of the scarlet Kangaroo Paw. Smiling solemnly, she decided on a quick cool shower, a bite to eat, then back to work. If she focused, she could have the book done sooner than she thought. Her muse was definitely working overtime.

Chapter Three

Damn, his cock was hard, and the lab-issued overalls he wore did nothing to hide it.

Mac shifted uncomfortably, his hand moving between his thighs to shift the heavy weight of his balls and palm the long length of his erection.

The woman had no modesty; that was all there was to it. She stood beneath the outdoor showerhead, turning slowly, her full, high breasts glistening with rivulets of water, the little rise of her tummy suntanned and wet, the patch of light blonde curls between her legs a contrast to the darker tone of her skin.

He frowned as his gaze centered there. He had always preferred a waxed mound to one hidden by the light covering of hair…until now. With Elyiana it appeared mysterious, tempting, it made him want to spread her luscious long legs and bury his head between them to reveal the secrets hidden there.

What secrets were hidden there, though? He fought the fog in his mind; he knew the answers were there, floating around somewhere, just out of reach. Did he know her? He felt he did, yet he could remember nothing about her. Not how she felt or how she tasted. He knew the sound of her voice, the lyrical accent that had him wanting to listen to her forever. Just as he knew she liked long, slow kisses, and that sex with her was always different.

Once in a jungle at dawn, another on his boardroom table. He shook his head. He knew her, he knew he did, but what he knew didn't make sense.

What had happened? How had he found himself on that gurney in an unfamiliar scientific lab? He knew when he woke up he had expected to see blood, and a lot of it But there had been none. Not a wound, not a scar, nothing to indicate the trauma he had somehow expected.

He ran his hand over his muscular abdomen now, frowning at the feel of it. He felt like himself, yet he didn't. He looked like himself, yet he didn't.

His hair shouldn't be so long, flowing past his shoulders in straight, dark red waves. It should be conservatively short. Yet, he knew he had once worn his hair just like this. He was stronger than he thought he should be. He had been going for three days, watching the house, making certain she was alone and that she wasn't being watched by any other than him. He had taken little more than a nap here or there, and yet he felt refreshed, at peak condition.

Only his mind wasn't functioning right. His brain felt scrambled. It was incredibly hard to remember the things he knew he should. Yet, he had known how to get out of the labs. Instinctively he had manipulated the security and the jet glider. He had found the switch that made the ultra-light air transport invisible to detection and had managed to disengage the GPS. How had he known how to do that yet couldn't remember things he should know about himself?

He was Mac. Thirty-five years old, rich, he knew he had money but not how to get to it. He had family, but he didn't know who they were. He knew he wasn't married, yet he felt he should be. He knew his life was in danger, but he couldn't remember how or why.

Goddamnit, why couldn't he put everything together? And why the hell did he feel equal parts arousal and fury for the woman he was watching?

He gritted his teeth as she took the soapy cloth, propped her slender long leg on a curved pipe and began to wash the honey gold mound of her pussy. Suds filled the sleek hair, dripping to the cement pad she stood on and hid the pink flesh he was dying to taste.

She would be sweet, like wild rain on his tongue. Yet, he couldn't remember going down on her to find out. He shook his head as she detached the showerhead from above, and lowered it until she could rinse the suds from between her golden thighs.

Her head fell back as obvious pleasure washed over her expression. The spray pelted her cunt, massaging her clit, and for a moment he thought he was going to come in his overalls at the sight of her little shiver of pleasure.

Elyiana. Her name whispered through his mind. Elyiana Richards.

Legs. He smiled at the thought. The woman had legs that went all the way to her neck. Long and shapely, perfectly rounded and strong. She could hold a man to her with legs like that. Wrap around him and hold him in place as he filled her with his seed.

His mind was consumed with thoughts of sex when he should be trying to figure out why the hell he was here and what this woman was to him. As she finished rinsing, he stood slowly to his feet, watching as she pulled the thin towel from the post beside her.

She wrapped it around her, tucking the ends securely between her breasts as she stared into the brush where he hid. He smiled tightly. She knew he was there. He didn't know how she knew, he hadn't done anything to give himself away and he knew it. But she was aware of him.

Mac tensed as she tilted her head, moving slowly, hesitantly as though to investigate the area he hid in. A frown crossed her brow and he could see a bit of confusion in her expression, as though she weren't certain. Frightened. He didn't want her frightened, he wanted her hot and screaming in pleasure beneath him as he worked his cock between her thighs, sliding into her creamy heat, working deep inside her tight pussy.

On the heels of that thought, the sound of an engine was heard overhead. Ducking further into the brush, he narrowed his eyes as the civilian jet glider set down in the cleared yard and a lanky male form exited the vehicle.

"Scott." Joy filled the woman's voice as she moved quickly to the craft, accepting the embrace that wrapped around her half naked body as though she were meant to be there.

Mac's teeth clenched as fury swept through him. Pure possessive rage tightened every muscle and bone in his body until it was all he could do to stay in place and watch the scene as it unfolded.

"Hey, gorgeous." The blond-haired Australian's accent was thick, filled with laughter as he dropped a quick kiss to the lips turned up to his. "Thought I'd check up on you before heading into Brisbane for supplies. You need anything while I'm out?"

"I'm still well stocked," her answer drifted back to him on the breeze. "Give me a call before you head back in, though, just in case."

He ruffled her hair affectionately before his arm dropped over her shoulders for another quick hug.

"Everything going fine then?" he asked her curiously. "How's the deadline?"

"Almost there." She backed up a bit, tightening the towel around her as the knot slipped. "We had another run in with *The* MacDougal though. The publisher has received several blistering emails this month alone. That man needs the stick pulled out of his arse in a bad way."

The MacDougal. The words echoed through his mind. He heard the disdain in her voice, the sense that she had somehow been hurt. Her expression was a bit pouty and a lot angry.

"So pull it out," the man laughed, a wide smile creasing his angular face. "If anyone could charm the beast that is The MacDougal, then you've surely taken my vote."

She chuckled at the comment. "But you're prejudiced in my favor," she reminded him.

"'Course I am." He shrugged, dropping a kiss to her forehead. "You charmed me, love. The MacDougal surely couldn't be any worse."

"Perhaps not worse, but not worth the effort," she assured him. "Now get out of here. I'm sure you're already running late. You're always running late."

"Running late I am," he agreed. "I'll give you a call in a few days. Have your list ready."

The door to the glider rose slowly and he ducked into the craft. With a quick wave as she stepped back, he closed the door. In a smooth surge of power, the small glider lifted then banked and shot into the sky.

With one last cautious glance toward where he hid, Elyiana moved quickly back to the safety of the house, closing the door behind her, and if he wasn't mistaken, locking it.

Was she frightened? Expecting him?

He gritted his teeth against the fragmented memories shifting through his brain, the scattering of impulses that had his frustration level rising. He needed answers and he was certain she had them. She had to have them or why else would every instinct and memory he could drag from his fractured mind send him here?

He wasn't going to find them here, skulking in the brush, watching the cheery comfort of the small house she had retreated inside. Besides, he was damned hungry, and thirst raged inside him, unlike anything he felt he had known before. He was confused but he was determined. This woman had to hold the answers he needed, why else would he be there. Why else would something inside him be pulling at him, pushing him closer to the woman who awaited him inside?

He wasn't the trusting sort, though, even for something as temping as the leggy little bohemian who had entered the house.

He slid purposely from the brush working his way around to the back of the little one-story bungalow to an opened bedroom window. He could hear her in the front of the house, the sound of her voice humming some tune, the muted sound of pots or pans banging in a cabinet.

Pushing the window open further, he climbed into the opening, straining to fit his muscular body through the small entrance. Once inside he moved quickly to the bedroom door, peeking through the small opening between it and the frame.

She had at least pulled on clothes, not that there was much to the dress she wore. The dark gold and violet sundress fell to just above her knees, swishing seductively along her trim legs.

The slender straps emphasized her graceful shoulders and long neck while her hair fell in a damp cascade of waves to the middle of her back.

He drew back as she turned to face the door, hearing her light footfalls as she headed for the bedroom. He tensed, knowing she was going to enter the room, that within moments, one way or the other, he was going to have her in his arms.

The door flew open and Mac moved. Using a speed he wasn't aware he possessed, he jerked her from her feet, pinning her back against his chest, her arms to her sides.

"Ye'll no be wanting to fight me," he warned darkly at her ear as her scream echoed around them both. "I willna hurt ye unless you make me, Legs. Please, for both our sakes, dinna make me."

For a moment, he thought she would obey him. That she would still in his arms and give him a chance to settle his senses and to control the lust raging through his body. But only for a moment.

One second he was holding a full-bodied, luscious little sex treat in his arms; the next minute he was attempting to still a fully enraged she-cat intent on de-manning him. Some nights, it just didn't pay to be a man.

Chapter Four

The rough material of his clothing did nothing to hide the thickness and length of his impressive shaft as it pressed hot and hard as the proverbial rock against the inside of her forearm. And quite impressive it was. In this situation however, her disconcertedness overshadowed her fascination. Lifting a brow, she flexed her fingers around his balls, which were of considerable size as well. Briefly she had struggled against her captor but quickly realized she was no match for his strength. Unable to move any other part of her body, she kicked back at his shins, but that seemed to garner no results whatsoever. So she was forced to resort to other tactics.

Over the years she had learned to heed her instincts. Never had they failed her or given her reason to doubt them. Now her instincts told her he wasn't going to harm her. His reaction was much like a wounded beast—defensive, confused. Still, it didn't sit well with her to be held against her will, and so efficiently too. She did feel compassion for him, but she just didn't like being manhandled and she wouldn't stand for it. Foolish man. She had her boundaries and if she was going to help him, he would respect them…one way or another.

A muscled forearm banded tightly across her chest just above her very responsive breasts holding her immobile against him. She let her free hand lightly skim down his arm and sunk her nails into his wrist. "This is all very Neanderthal, don't you think?" Just for emphasis she tightened her grip on his balls, smiling as he growled in response.

Pulling her tighter against his side, he leaned down closer to her ear. There was nothing soft about him. Delightfully her nipples tightened with every warm breath that fanned her neck. Cheeky girls, they had always been overly responsive to any remotely provocative stimulation and they had really bad timing. It was her recent frame of mind that was to blame. Her mind had been on seduction, surrender, lust. Add to all of that, this man was beyond provocative, he was sex walking. It wasn't as though she didn't find his big hard body tantalizing.

The nice package she clutched in her palm and the steely cock that now pulsed against her arm were extremely arousing. Had the circumstances been much different than the one she found herself in now, she might have liked getting to know him and possibly would have been interested in investigating his endowments and whatever else he had to offer. But she hadn't met him under other circumstances. He'd forced his way in and made her feel like a victim in her own home. That was wholly unacceptable.

"Who else is in the house?" he grumbled, his lips close to her ear.

Growing more impatient with him, Elyiana tightened her grip, her voice lowered. "There's no one in the house but me. Now let me go or I'll rip them off," she warned.

"If you're lying to me, I'll ha' your wee neck snapped before ye can think to twist your wrist."

Believing that he could do whatever he willed was no problem but still she wasn't afraid, just highly irritated and heading rapidly toward angry. "You willing to take that chance, mate?" she gritted out as she jerked lightly. He yanked her hard against him causing the air to leave her lungs in a whoosh as he lowered his head, his lips brushing her ear.

"I'm no playin' wi' ye, woman."

"I am not lying to you." She breathed hoarsely, frustrated with the mingling arousal and fury she felt. The throbbing of her heart wildly pumping blood through her veins grew loud in her ears.

"Loosen ye grip on my stones." A shiver ran up her spine at the low rumbling command.

And she did, slowly; very slowly she uncurled her fingers as he loosened his hold and she gasped for breath.

But she didn't let her hand drop. Instead she let her hand test the feel of his shaft, sliding upward through the thick material. "Better?" She purred.

"That'll no keep you safe either, lass." His voice had gone husky and dark. "I'm going to release you. Like I said. Dinna make me hurt ye."

Finally dropping his arms from around her, she turned and looked up into his face. Wow, he was beautiful. Much taller than she, he gazed down, assessing her with his deep forest green eyes. He looked much like a fierce yet dignified lion, with his thick mane of red-gold hair framing his extremely handsome face and hanging past his shoulders in waves, perfectly smooth, tanned skin, high cheekbones, straight regal nose, and a very well-crafted mouth. Full lips, firm enough to make a woman want to run her tongue over them. Flawless, almost too flawless.

Ah yes, this man was a masterpiece, most assuredly made in God's own image. The artist in her couldn't resist putting him into a scene in one of her books. After all he had shown himself to be an uber-alpha. Big, sexy as hell as well as forceful, dogmatic, dangerous. Mmm, just perfect, she thought with a frown. Maybe she'd change up his looks a bit. Describe his face with a bit more angles, rough around the edges, maybe even give him an intriguing scar or something.

In her mind she could see the scene play out. Naked, rising over her, his very substantial erection probing the swollen folds of her soaked pussy as those sensuous lips sucked at her eager nipple. The images had her nipples straining even more than they were already, her channel walls clench with hungry need to be filled. She bit her lip and breathed deeply as her imagination bathed her body in hot liquid pleasure.

That must be why he seemed so familiar she thought, narrowing her eyes, because he's so similar to the heroes in the many novels she'd written. The MacDougal. He did resemble the MacDougal, she thought, her eyes widening as she studied his face, but not completely. His hair was too long, too light, eyes too dark. His nose was different, so was his jawline and chin. Wow. Evidently she had been fantasizing way too much about The MacDougal lately.

He narrowed his eyes in return and tilted his head. "Are you all right? You seem a bit afflicted. I didna hurt you, did I?"

Lost in her erotic thoughts she paused, taking a deep breath and forced herself to withdraw from them, set them aside 'til she could get back to her manuscript. Dear God, she should have finished what she started on the beach, she thought with exasperation. With a sigh she smiled up at him and resisted the urge to laugh. If wanting to fuck him dry was an affliction then yes, she was afflicted in a major way.

Very aware of him, his energy, she just didn't pick up anything that should make her feel threatened. Intuitively she knew he was no danger to her. "Just my pride. I'm fine. Were you looking to steal something? Do you need money?"

His eyes cut back to hers in surprise, his body stiffened, his frown deepened. Slowly he shook his head. "Of course not."

"All right." Evidently he's a bit uptight, she thought, arching a brow.

"You live alone then?" he asked, glancing over her shoulder, his sharp green eyes narrowing slightly.

"Yep. Look, are you hungry?" She'd been going to make dinner when he showed up and started acting like a cross between a serial killer and an overprotective big brother. Looking up, she was taken aback by the feral look on his rugged face. Damn, she had to either shake this wicked lust or knock him on his ass and rape him. What in the world had come over her? Being caught up in the eroticism of her story was nothing new but there was something about this man that drove her crazy.

"Who was the pup wi' his hands all over you earlier?" The anger clear in his tone had her lifting a brow.

"Pup? What pup…oh! Do you mean Scott?" To his scowl, she grinned. "That's funny, although I don't believe he'd find humor in the title."

"Are ye fucking him?"

"Whoa." Elyiana frowned, her humor instantly evaporating. "Not that it's any of your business but seeing how you're the one with the power..." she snarled at him. "Scott is my best friend."

"I asked ye if you fuck him." The tension between them spiked as he crowded her.

"We pleasure each other on occasion." She answered a bit too quickly as apprehension slithered through her.

The muscle in his jaw pulsed, his green eyes had gone dark, almost emerald with fury. "You'll no be *pleasuring* your fuck buddy anymore."

Oh, now that was too much.

"Bloody hell?! And just what do you think gives you the right to tell me who I can and cannot fuck?" she ranted, stabbing him in the chest with her nail.

Long fingers held her face in a grip tight enough to make his point, but not harsh enough to leave a mark. "I'll no share ye. No wi' anyone." His eyes flashed with fury, his voice was a low growl.

The man was supercilious, pompous, egocentric, or worse, deranged. Her chest rose and fell with indignation. The unmitigated gall! The sheer audacity! It was irrational, her anger, but no more irrational than his staking a claim on her after he'd just broken into her home and took her captive.

Dammit, she was trying to be nice. Understanding.

"What gives you the idea that you have any right to me at all?" She turned her head away, dislodging her face from his grip. Fury seared her veins as she met his savage gaze, daring him. "No one. Do you hear me? No one has any claim on me. I'm not property, you bastard. Where are you from anyway, the Dark Ages? You don't even know me."

But as she stared up at him she couldn't help but notice the confusion swirling in his eyes. He seemed to struggle to understand and part of her wanted to reach out to him because of it, just as another part of her wanted to punch him in the stomach. Really hard. And yet another part...*oh hell, forget that part, you horny vixen,* she told herself. For now. First the male needed an education.

"Hell, I don't even know your name," she snapped.

He blinked at her a couple of times as though her statement surprised him. Although she couldn't think of why it should.

"Mac." He scowled, stating his name with cool authority.

Again she rolled her eyes at him. Wherever he'd come from he was used to being unquestionably obeyed. Poor man was going to be sorely disappointed. She bowed to no one. Least of all some oversized brute who doesn't know how to use the door.

"Well, Mac, I'm Elyiana. If you need a place to stay, you can have the couch. I was just about to fix dinner." She turned and walked from the bedroom into the kitchen.

"Have ye any idea how dangerous it is to be out alone?" he scolded her sharply, following fast on her heels, giving her no space.

Strange, really she ought to be nervous, frightened of someone she didn't know invading her home, invading her space. But she wasn't afraid at all.

"I can take care of myself, but thanks for your concern," she said, amused.

If it were dangerous for her to be alone then she'd been in danger for most of her adult life. A gentle pain nudged at her heart remembering the loving parents she'd lost to a freak auto accident. Barely in her teens, she'd had no one else. No grandparents, no siblings. Her aunts and uncles had dusted their feet of her parents long ago as well as herself by default. Her mum and dad had been very active in the alternative lifestyle Nimbin, Australia offered. They adored Elyiana and wanted to raise their only daughter free of the restrictive mindset of an economically and politically driven society.

With love abundant and schooling her at home in more than just the "three Rs", they had succeeded in equipping her with all she needed to not only survive but thrive on her own. Self-assured and motivated, she'd been perfectly capable of caring for herself. Neighbors looked in on her from time to time. The authority of Nimbin didn't make an issue of the fourteen-year-old girl making it on her own.

There had been enough money left to sustain her. She didn't need much and the excess from her organic garden as well as the veggies and jams she preserved always sold very well. Wanting to be closer to the ocean, she moved southward closer to Byron Bay when she turned eighteen. There wasn't a great difference between Nimbin and Byron Bay as far as the culture and community was concerned. She continued her gardening and was just as well received in her new town. Even now that she made an excellent living writing, she kept up the bottling. Only now, she just gave away what she didn't use herself.

It might have been nice to have someone around. A warm pair of arms to wrap up in, to lean on, but she felt she'd coped well. Even though her parents were no longer bound to the earth, to their physical bodies, Elyiana knew they were with her always. Without a doubt, she knew. There were nights when she felt especially melancholy and missed them so much her head ached from it, but she could feel her mother with her, the ever so slight brush of an unseen hand against her cheek, and it gave her peace. Never sure what to call the perceptions, she'd shrugged it off, just considering herself especially in tune with her instincts. They had never misled her and she never took them for granted. In her opinion any psychic ability, no matter how slight, was a gift from God.

Maybe He knew she would need the heightened intuition, the ability to discern things beyond those bound by logic and the physical in order to survive. Regardless of why she was blessed with the gift, she was thankful for it. It let her still feel connected, to some extent, to her mum and dad. That connection, at times, was all that got her through. Maybe that's why she wasn't afraid. She knew there were those in the spirit world looking out for her. Protecting her. And she wasn't afraid to die. Not that she was ready to leave this dimension yet, she just wasn't afraid of passing over when it was time for her to go. Without a doubt, she knew her mother and father waited for her there.

Swallowing the fresh emotion, she pushed the memories away and turned her attention back to the man invading her space. He was an enigma. There was little she could discern from him. Though she knew right away he wouldn't harm her, she knew he wasn't harmless. He was very controlled, restrained. It would be absolutely delicious to find out just what it took to make the big man fall to his knees and lose that iron-fisted control.

Finding out what happened when all that furious anger turned into heated passion was an intriguing prospect. This haughty, protective caveman attitude however, was something she would not tolerate. Not from him, or anyone else. His gazed traveled over her body, condescension clear in the arrogant green pools, but he said no more. Not out loud, anyway. His expression spoke volumes. With a shrug, she focused on preparing her food.

Closing the distance between them, he took the plates from her and set them aside. With that same mixture of irritation and fascination he'd had in his eyes all evening, he gazed down at her. She felt the heat pulse from his body and watched the forest green of his eyes darken and dilate. Before she could slip away, one arm wrapped around her waist and crushed her to him. Taking possession, his mouth covered hers as his head tilted slightly giving him better access.

Cupping her face with his free hand, his thumb caressed in little circles at the corner of her mouth, urging her mouth open to give him better access. She forgot to breathe as his tongue delved between her lips just enough to tease, to taste. It felt as though flames licked through her veins. *It's only a kiss for God's sake, Elyiana,* she told herself. But her body didn't give a damn.

Finally she surrendered to the flash fire of need that came to life inside her. On a lusty moan she opened to him, her tongue meeting his. Her hands slid up his chest to graze his pebble-hard nipples, then higher to comb through his long hair, holding his mouth to hers as she pressed tighter against him. Backwards, they were moving back she realized just as her back came up against the wall. His mouth began a slow trek down her jaw to her neck, his teeth nipping at her as his thigh pushed her legs apart and pressed against the heat of her.

Elyiana whimpered as he ripped her dress exposing a breast. The pleasure bloomed bright inside her as the muscled walls of her pussy contracted, tightening at the onslaught of his voracious mouth, biting and sucking at one breast while his hand kneaded the other, his thumb and finger squeezing her nipple, his hard thigh grinding against the swollen lips of her cunt.

"Mac," she groaned. "Wait. Mac."

Damn it, she couldn't breathe, and her channel tightened so fiercely it hurt. But, dear God, he felt good and if the situation were different she would go with it. But there were some things that needed clearing up first. It would be best if she knew where he'd come from, what he was hiding from first. And she had to be assured that he understood sex gave him no rights to her.

"What is it, Legs?" His dark husky voice like a deep caress rumbled through her. "Do ye no like this?" His hand cupped her pussy. "Or this?" He sucked hard on her nipple as he slid a finger over her wet slit through her panties. Her head fell back on a whimper, all rational thought deserted her, and her body trembled under his hands.

"No," she sobbed "oh…hell, yes."

Her hands fisted in the material of his overalls. Logic warred with pure desire and she was quickly becoming aware of which was winning out. Struggling to catch her breath she ran her hands over the overalls he wore.

She finally acquiesced. "Come to my room." Unzipping, unsnapping and unbuttoning the damned suit 'til finally it fell in a puddle on the floor. Hungry to touch his skin, her hands roamed over his arms to his chest, down his stomach to wrap around the incredible width of him. Gasping she looked up at him. "Take me to bed, Mac. Take me to bed and fuck me," she pleaded, pressing her body to him, her thumb gliding over the tip of his cock.

"I'll no make it to the bed," he groaned.

In the living room, the viewing screen flashed to life.

"...is The MacDougal missing, or worse, could he be dead?" The news anchor's practiced voice sang from the viewing screen's speakers.

Mac froze with his hand fisted in the waistband of Elyiana's silk panties.

"Wha—?" Elyiana fought to catch her breath. "Mac?"

"Hush."

She followed his gaze, the sensual fog surrounding her clearing abruptly. Breathlessly, she pushed Mac gently and put some space between them.

"We'll have the full report for you when we return..." the anchor teased as the news cut to a commercial.

She'd set the timer, otherwise she'd never remember to watch the news and she had to watch the news. This night, however, it was an intrusion, or her salvation...she wasn't sure. Most every night The MacDougal was sure to be interviewed or quoted or talked about in one way or other. The man provided such comic relief with his staunch appearance and antiquated ideas he was a must-see. She enjoyed using him in her novels at times. Her original plan had been make him the villain but there was just something very sensual about him, raw sexuality that wouldn't be denied. Therefore, she let the character guide her.

Most of the times when she had used him in a novel, she'd been very subtle about it. But then somehow he got suspicious and evidently read most of her books. The more he fought her, the more obvious she'd become, 'til this last book she so obviously portrayed him as the hero that it couldn't be overlooked. If asked during an interview, she'd never admitted to it even though she didn't really deny it either. Never had she written anything slanderous or defamatory.

In one novel, he was a corporate lawyer brought down from his arrogant pedestal by the love of a strong and courageous woman. In another, she'd used him to create a mercenary, fighting to keep his woman alive in the brutal jungle. It was the Scottish Laird she liked the best however, because it most fit him, she guessed.

"It must be six o'clock," she panted.

It was true that she didn't like The MacDougal. Hell, she opposed nearly everything he believed in. Still she didn't want him dead. Of course, he wasn't dead. She shrugged off the flicker of apprehension that coursed through her. The man was rock-solid, indestructible. When it was time for *The* MacDougal to die, he would plan a press conference and let everyone know when, how and where, and just what he required the world to think about it. No, The MacDougal wasn't dead. The man was too arrogant to die.

She couldn't help but frown as Mac glanced at her before bending to pull the overalls up, his erection still very much at the prime. His complete distraction was more than a little unnerving. Oh well, some people thought the sun rose and fell in The MacDougal's ass. She sighed and with a shrug she turned away from him. "I think Scott left some clothes in my room. I'll go see."

With her body still humming from her unsatisfied arousal, and her mind cluttered with too many unanswered questions, Elyiana went to her bedroom to change her soaked panties and put on her favorite overlong, ultra-soft, cotton nightshirt. Still the material rubbed against her taut nipples and made her want to scream. She grabbed the pair of shorts Scott had left but couldn't find a shirt. The shorts were made of knit material so hopefully Mac could make them fit.

In the living room he stood beside her favorite chair, his arms folded over his chest, his legs braced apart, his cock at full mast tenting his overalls.

"...official word at this point in time is that The MacDougal will be on a much needed retreat at an undisclosed location for an unspecified span of time..."

"*THE* MacDougal, as if he were a dominion all unto himself," she snorted to herself. There, she knew he wasn't dead. "I guess *The* MacDougal needed some downtime. I suppose his arse was chapped from everyone kissing it."

"Shhh, be still." Mac said sharply, his brows furrowed as he focused on the screen before them. Listening to every word. And she couldn't help rolling her eyes.

Chapter Five

Absently, Mac pulled the dull green suit back up his body and buttoned it as he watched the television with a sense of nervous energy. The pounding lust hadn't completely abated from his body. His dick was still rock-hard, but his attention was held by the report on the screen rather than the woman mumbling sarcastically from the doorway to her bedroom.

He couldn't blame her for being upset. She had been wild and wet, as ready for him as he was for her. But this was more important at the moment. Why, he wasn't certain.

He would take her, soon. There was no question of it. But the news held his attention rapt at the moment. The young woman speaking had the fragmented memories in his head shifting, surging, creating a buzz in his ears that he found not at all natural.

"...MacDougal needs to vacation sometime, gentleman." A stately redhead stood in front of the cameras, a cool smile on her lips, her emerald green eyes cold as ice.

He should know those eyes, he thought. He should know that woman.

"Miss MacDougal, your brother has so far missed two very important Coalition meetings as well as his own personal fundraiser, and you say he's merely taking downtime?" one reporter sneered. "And what about the report that a bloody MacDougal was seen being transported to a secret lab outside Dresden? There are reports that The MacDougal is dead."

She was bloody fuckin' going to kill that bastard, Mac thought in some amusement before a frown snapped into place. Why would he be so certain the woman facing the cameras would be so bloodthirsty?

For a moment, a muted sound, rather like bees buzzing, echoed in his ears as he felt a sensation rather like electricity moving through his brain. He stilled, attempting to isolate and explain the feeling, but just as quickly, it was gone.

"You like to live dangerously don't you?" he heard Miss MacDougal comment to the reporter softly, a slow, cold smile shaping her generous lips as her green eyes narrowed on the reporter. "If this was true, never doubt there wouldn't be more than The MacDougal's death to report. There would be that of his assassin as well as the pack of hungry reporters dogging his every step," she said pointedly, her Scots brogue thickening her voice just enough to make it noticeable. "Interview's over, children. Go outside and play now. I have work to do."

Mac had to restrain his grin. Damn, she was cold as ice, and madder than hell. For a moment, he felt a sense of affection tighten his chest before the memory that sparked it seemed to fade from existence.

"Now that is a woman that needs to seriously relax and regroup. Look at her eyes, she's sad. There's something about her eyes that's positively heartbreaking," Elyiana said softly behind him. "I've said she could use a good fucking, but I think it's more a case of needing more loving."

He grunted in irritation. He hated to admit it, and he didn't know why, but she was right. There was something shadowed about the woman's eyes, a sadness that made his heart clench each time he glimpsed it.

The buzzing in his head returned, causing his skull to feel as though it was tightening, his body to clench with tension. It was unlike anything he could ever remember feeling before. But just as quickly as it began, it was gone again.

"The MacDougal, I'm certain, will answer all your questions when he returns from his vacation." A tall, dark-haired man stepped to the podium, his black eyes piercing and intelligent, his voice controlled and chillingly polite. "As you've seen in the past, he is prone to striking absences as it suits his mood. I assure you, there are no dead, bloody bodies that we're hiding."

He was lying. Mac felt it to the bottom of his soul.

"Now there is a work of art we don't get to see very often," the leggy little sprite behind him cooed with more interest than Mac deemed appropriate. "Tael McLeod. He's a very distant relative of MacDougal as I understand it. Personally, I think he's the most charming of the three. What do you think?"

Mac turned back to her slowly. She stood, propped against the doorway, her purple, black and platinum hair falling over her shoulders and tempting his fingers to tangle within it again.

"The three of what?" he asked her, attempting to rein in his demand for answers and to attempt polite curiosity instead.

She rolled her eyes expressively.

"The MacDougal, his sister Amareth was the ice queen giving the interview. The man you just saw was Tael McLeod, a distant relative. What planet are you from anyway? Everyone old enough to speak or listen knows the MacDougal main family. They're almost as popular as the once-reigning Royal Family was."

He shook his head faintly. "I dinna know what you meant." He attempted a placating smile, but by her frown he imagined it fell a wee bit short.

He restrained his larger grin, realizing that irritating her was a most pleasant diversion from the confusion buzzing around in his head.

"Hmm," she murmured a bit mockingly, her gaze flickering to the bulge that was paining him more than he wanted to admit. Dammit, he'd never been so hard, so damned horny around a woman in his life.

"So are you related?" She tipped her head, her strange, violet-colored eyes watching him closely.

He stared back at her silently, arching his brow to indicate his uncertainty at her question. Related to what? His hard, hard dick? Damn fickle flesh was making him crazy to fuck her. He couldn't understand it; she obviously had no clue who he was. He had no clue who he was. So why did he feel as though he knew her?

"To the MacDougal Clan," she explained patiently. "Are you related to them? You seem to have many of the same features. They're pretty striking."

Was he?

He shrugged his shoulders nonchalantly. "I've no clue." No truer words were ever spoken.

"Boy, you're just full of information tonight aren't you?" She finally shook her head in irritation.

He wanted to chuckle, but restrained the impulse.

"And aren't you just full of questions," he shot back. "Lass, you'd fair wear a man out with that mouth of yours. I could suggest other uses rather than harassin' him with questions if you're of a mind to cooperate."

Her eyes narrowed. She wasn't angry, but he got the feeling she didn't much care for his tone of voice either. She was a striking balance between strength and womanly softness. A dreamer, yet a fighter. She intrigued him, made him want to learn more than just the varied sexual positions he thought he could remember her in.

Dammit, this was irritating. The flashes of memory didn't feel like memory, but they were there all the same. Where had they come from?

"Hmphf, wouldn't surprise me a bit if you were a really close relation." She tossed her hair over her shoulder, regarding him with a delicate frown. "You're arrogant enough."

"And you're mouthy enough," he snapped back, flexing his shoulders as he fought the tension filling him.

This had gone on too long now. It had been three bloody days since his escape from the lab, strangely enough, in Germany, and there were still no answers to be found in the chaos of his brain.

She smiled then, a slow sultry curve of her lips that had him wanting to growl with the overriding lust that began to pour through his body. Her pouty lips called to mind images he couldn't explain. Her sweetly curved, luscious little body made him want to howl with hunger.

She moved closer to him, her breasts swaying beneath the thin nightshirt she had changed into. If he remembered correctly, he had perhaps ruined the dress she had worn in the kitchen.

"You're gonna get fucked, lass, if you keep pushing me in this manner," he finally warned her with what he considered an amazing amount of self-control.

Her eyes filled with laughter as she brushed past him. He almost smiled in response.

"I believe I might have offered the use of my bed earlier," she reminded him with a soft little laugh.

And did she make such an offer often to strange men? he wondered.

"A bit easy aren't you, darlin?" he snarled, consumed with anger at the thought of another man touching her.

Her eyes narrowed just enough to show he had managed to prick that cool façade she kept wrapped around her like a shield of protection. Her slight body stiffened, but a smile shaped her lips. A bit mocking, a bit tight.

"Maybe, but you weren't all that hard to get yourself…darlin'," she replied with cool disdain as she moved to the small desk set in the corner of the room.

The living room of the small bungalow was a lot like the woman. It held an odd assortment of displays on the walls. Framed prints of the planet at another time, a time before the wars that took so many lives.

There was one of the much-heralded World Trade Center, before its destruction. The Eiffel Tower before it was blown to a mound of twisted rubble nearly a century later. The Statue of Liberty, God bless her heart, before she was moved to a safer place. The old Sydney Opera House, the original, before its new, ultramodern design replaced the wreckage that a bomb had made of it.

He might not know who he was, but Mac was more than a little pleased to see that parts of his memory were in working order. And he might not remember his personal history, but he knew much of world history.

There were glass-enclosed cases of paperback books that looked too old to actually exist. No one read paperback anymore. Why would they want to?

The furniture was wide, and thickly cushioned. A couch and several chairs, real wood tables and small, old-fashioned lamps. Behind the antique desk was a round, cushioned swivel chair that he could imagine her curled within, either reading or working on whatever she did at the desk.

Elyiana Richards wasn't a woman who appeared to enjoy the comforts of civilization. The furniture didn't automatically adjust to body size or weight, and the floor was made of sanded wood rather than the cushioned comfort of the new lighter grade of artificial planks.

She was still watching him a bit mockingly, her violet eyes nearly glowing with ire at the thought that he would call her to task for her free-spirited sexuality. He shouldn't give a damn who she fucked, but he did, and that made no sense.

He wanted to grab her and shake her and demand the answers to the questions rising in his brain. He wanted to know why he knew her, yet she watched him as though he were a stranger. Why did he hunger for her with a lust he felt it would take years to sate, when he knew entanglements were something he didn't want, nor had he desired. Or did he? Goddammit it!

He raked his fingers through his hair, grimacing in irritation at the long strands that had a habit of framing his face much too closely.

"Look, I have work to do," she finally snapped. "You can sleep on the couch or in the bedroom, doesn't matter to me which. I laid a pair of shorts out on the bed for you, if you would like to see if they fit. Just stay out of my way. I don't have the time or the inclination to educate you on just how arrogant and archaic your ideas are right now. You could give that damned MacDougal a run for his money."

He frowned at the insolence in her voice and the note of irritation. He wanted to berate her further for simply daring to speak to him in such a manner. He had a feeling he could be allowing a dangerous precedent to be set in letting her get away with it.

"You donna like The MacDougal?" He crossed his arms over his chest as he regarded her with a spark of amusement. "He's a rather important man, wouldn't you say?"

"He's a rather arrogant arse is what I would say," she muttered as she took a seat behind the desk and regarded him with a frosty stare as she hit a key on the flat keypad on the desk, instantly bringing up the hologram screen she obviously worked on.

"Sounds as though you know him well?" He lifted a brow in question.

"Not likely," she snorted. "*The MacDougal* doesn't associate with the likes of me, I would imagine. A little too down to earth for *His Highness* to be bothered with."

The MacDougal sounded like a fool, but Mac rather thought perhaps the little spitfire across the room might not know as much as she thought she did.

"And that sister of his isn't much better." She leaned back in her chair, continuing her dissertation of the MacDougal family. "Amareth MacDougal is the head of his highness' security. She'd rather put a bullet in a man than fuck him. Tael McLeod is a bit nicer from what I've seen, but he's still a MacDougal jerk. The crown castle of the Clan MacDougal is one of the few ancient castles that weren't decimated during the planetary war and he's richer than Midas. Personally I think the sister isn't as hard as she makes herself out to be, but I would have to get closer to her to be certain. That MacDougal gets on my last nerve though. I think he needs someone to knock him off his little pedestal."

"And you think you can?" he asked her curiously, more amused than he was willing to let her see.

She smiled that sexy smile, her violet eyes heating with laughter. He loved that look, he realized. Part pixie, part temptress, her pouty little mouth curved with enticing humor, the way her eyes sparkled with warmth and the remnants of arousal.

"He just needs a good fuck. A nice, long, drawn-out, slow burning fuck that curls his toes and makes him forget all about that superman control he likes to let people see." Her voice became huskier, hungrier when she said the words.

Mac frowned darkly at her demeanor. She wanted him, The MacDougal that was. He could see it in her eyes, hear it in her voice. And he refused to allow it to continue. Slowly he advanced on her, moving until he stood before her, bending over her, his eyes piercing into the laughter-filled depths of hers.

"As long as he's no fuckin' you," he hissed, watching the instant surprise that washed over her expression. "If you want to burn, darlin', or make another, then you can come to me. But you dare try to make me share you with another, and your arse will be so sore for so damned long you won't be able to sit, let alone fuck another man. Remember that one."

She stared back at him in surprise. "You're crazy, right? Just my luck to get stuck with a crazy man. Look, Mac, I don't know you and I'm starting to not want to know you. You're arrogant and bossy and too damned manipulative for your own good. What matters right now, is finding out why you're here. Something you haven't exactly explained so far. Would you like to try?"

The mocking inquiry on her face, the laughing little tilt to her lips and the amused indulgence in her eyes grated on his nerves. The little hellion thought she could control him? Thought she could turn him away from why he was there.

Why was he there, dammit? It made no sense that he was there to claim her and to save her. There was a danger around him that he couldn't place, and he was determined it wouldn't touch her. She was his, and he knew enough about himself to know that he wasn't insane. Merely determined. That she didn't know him didn't matter. He knew he had claimed her long before this, and as he saw it, that was all that mattered.

He shook his head slowly. "No, lass, what matters right now is kissing you. Kissing you and making certain that when ye think of a man, it's me you're thinking of. Now, get familiar with this, Legs."

This wasn't like him, Mac knew it, but he couldn't help what he did next. His hands gripped her slender shoulders as he ignored the surprise in her eyes and pulled her from her chair, holding her firmly to his chest before his head lowered.

She gasped. A sweet female sound that he knew he had never heard before. Wariness, heat and hunger filled the sound a second before he captured her lips, parting them swiftly and sending his tongue seeking the unique flavor he knew she would possess.

He should have been more concerned with answering the questions rioting inside his brain before she appeared, but one look at those long legs and all he could think about was having them wrapped around his hips. Clinging to him, holding him to her as he worked every inch of his cock up her tight, hot pussy. And she was hot. He knew she was hot.

Her kiss was like a firestorm itself. A strangled moan vibrated against his lips as she gave in to him, her hands gripping his shoulders, holding tight to him as her lips and tongue began to feed from his kiss.

His arms wrapped around her, holding her close, feeling the warmth of her against him, those long legs moving against his, parting for his thigh as it wedged between them.

Heat burst against his flesh as it met the damp mound of her pussy. Her nightshirt slid above her thighs, the flowing fabric not hindering him in the slightest as he pressed her tight against him. God, she was exquisite. So hot and silky, smelling of sunshine and life, something he realized he hadn't smelled in a very long time.

His hands moved from her back to her rear, cupping the delicate curves, his fingers clenching in the taut flesh as he pulled her closer to him, moving her, forcing her to ride the hard muscles of his thigh.

"Damn, you're hot," he groaned, forcing his lips from her so he could caress the graceful line of her jaw, the smooth arch of her neck. "Sweet and intoxicating. You go to my head, Ellie. Like nothing I've ever known, you make me drunk on your taste."

No other woman had done this. He knew that, felt it to the soles of his feet. No other woman had ever made him burn as he now burned. No other woman had ever touched his soul as this one did, and it infuriated him that she didn't seem to know him. That she didn't have the memories he did of taking her, holding her, loving her.

And God help him, he did need to love her. He could feel that need tightening his muscles, searing his mind with the overriding demand that he take her now. Possess her, mark her forever as his own. Just his…

"Burn with me, Ellie, " he demanded as his lips feathered down her neck, growing ever closer to the full, swollen mounds of her breasts where they pressed above the bodice of her loose nightdress. "Now."

He nudged aside the material, his fingers moving quickly on the tiny buttons that held it together, determined to hold the fragile weight of her breasts in his hands, to taste the sweetness of her hard nipples against his lips.

"This is insane," she cried out, though she made no move to fight against him.

Better yet, when his tongue swiped over the berry ripeness of the hard point, she jerked at the touch, moaning with sensual pleasure as her hands threaded into his hair, pressing him closer.

"How sweet you are." He was breathing hard, lust riding him in a way he knew he had never experienced before. "So sweet and hot, Ellie, that you make me crazy."

He couldn't get enough of her taste. His tongue curled around the hard point of her nipple as his mouth covered it, drawing on her firmly as little kittenish cries began to echo around him.

"Yes," she hissed erotically then, her body becoming supple, pliant, as his mouth sucked at the tender peak. "Harder, Mac. Do it harder."

He moaned at the demand, he couldn't help it. The sound of it went straight to his cock, spilling a small amount of fluid from its tip as the need began to overwhelm him. His. This woman, this moment in time, it was all his…

Chapter Six

Passion exploded. She could swear she heard the energy crackling, sizzling as it arced between them. Urgently she speared her fingers into his hair and held his head closer to her breast. Even the coarse texture of his thick, red-gold hair against her fingertips, her palm, intensified the starbursts of arousal firing through her, spurring her desire, driving out all logic, all reason.

Larger than life, he overwhelmed her and she gladly surrendered. Using his teeth, his tongue, he nearly drove her over the edge. No, she wanted him closer; he wasn't nearly close enough. Biting her lip, she fought to keep from rubbing her aching flesh against his thigh. Already she felt engorged, slippery wet and blazing hot. The slightest friction would throw her into a climax and she wasn't ready. Not yet.

"Mmm, Mac." She moaned, fisting her hands in his hair.

Her thoughts were scrambled. Nothing mattered but the feel of him, his big hands cupping her ass, his long fingers caressing, spreading her open. As he lifted her, his fingers probing, caressing the sensitive crevice where her ass and her pussy met, she gasped, releasing his hair from her death grip, and clung to his shoulders. She felt herself being lowered onto the plush couch, heard the ripping of material as he tore her silk panties from her body.

"*Tha thu brèagha,*" he murmured the breathy words huskily against her neck, nuzzling her with his nose before lifting her nightdress over her head and tossing it aside. "So beautiful." He groaned.

Like a vortex, the emotions, the sensations, swept her up as his hands slid up over her body relieving her of the rest of her clothing.

Hands so hot she thought she'd burst into flames at any moment, cupped and lifted her breasts and nipped at the inner swells and underneath. Licking and sucking, he avoided her nipples this time, making her crazy with need. Yearning for release but wanting the euphoria to never end, she struggled to breathe, to concentrate, to control the building tension. This experience was beyond anything she'd ever read about, or written about and far more erotic than she'd ever experienced, and she wanted to draw it out, make it last forever. But, dear God, if he didn't touch her pussy soon she thought she would scream from the intensity.

As if he read her mind, his hand skimmed down her body over her hips to her thighs. Gripping them gently, he kneaded them, slowly urging them apart as his mouth made its way down the front of her body. Clenching her teeth, her head fell back on a whimper. His thumbs made wide firm circles on her inner thighs, working upward toward the sodden heat of her. Warm breath fanned her hypersensitive skin as he took his time, pausing at her navel to tease her with his tongue and teeth.

Sure she would die from the sheer pleasure, she cried out as his thumbs barely grazed the swollen outer lips of her pussy. "Oh please, Mac," she cried.

Raising his head, he met her gaze, his brows knit together in a struggle for control as well. He pressed her legs open wider and kissed his way down her body, using his teeth, his tongue, as he wrenched soft throaty cries from deep inside her. Blowing gently, he ruffled the soft thatch of hair shielding her cunt before spreading her lips slowly. Her lips parted on a moan as he kept his eyes locked with hers, his tongue delving inside her folds, licking upward to flick over her clit.

"*Mo milis rós,*" he whispered. "Bloom for me, baby." Dark and lusty, his voice rumbled against her.

Her breath came in short, soft pants as he leaned her back against the soft cushions. Achingly slow, he played her like an instrument of pleasure. His hands smoothed up her body and cupped her breasts, squeezing her nipples as he began to kiss, lick in earnest.

"Incredible. Ellie, you're petal-soft. So fucking sweet." He breathed against her pussy as he spread her open with his tongue, careful to avoid her clit. Her heart hammered against her chest in rhythm with each stroke of his tongue, pushing her closer, forcing her upward. Smoothly he thrust one finger inside her pulsing vagina.

Ah, that felt so good. She hadn't realized how hungry she had been, how desperate she was to be filled with him. Clutching at him, she cried out for more.

Withdrawing and thrusting again, he added another finger, stretching her, caressing her inner walls as they began to spasm, clutching at them. The pleasure gathered, her cunt clenching harder as she bore down.

Crying out, she moved her hips against his mouth as he devoured her. "Oh yes, Mac, harder."

Like a man starving to death, he ravaged her. Gently, he used his teeth, alternately nibbling at her outer lips, her inner more sensitive flesh. Spreading her legs wider to give him better access, she looked down, watching him consume her. It was the most erotic thing she'd ever seen.

The sheer ecstasy of it would kill her, she was sure of it, but she didn't care. Her heart pounded so furiously against her ribs she thought any minute it would explode.

When his lips closed over her clit, sucking hard, drawing it in as his tongue rasped firmly over the distended nub, her mind shattered, her body trembled, convulsed. Her head fell back as a scream of ecstasy was ripped from her. Unabashedly she swiveled her hips against his mouth. For a split second she forgot to breathe as the exquisite pleasure/pain gripped her, held her, before shattering her into a million bright sensations. Still he sucked her, stroked her spasming cunt as he cupped her ass holding her still as she felt another orgasm building.

Faster, it grew and exploded within her again as she gripped the upholstery of the sofa cushions. The sharp peak stole her breath, her sanity. He rose up on his knees then, his hands roaming over her back, pulling her hips closer to the edge.

As she shuddered through the aftershocks of her latest climax, he wedged himself between her thighs. Delirious with her need for more she clutched at him pulling at the damn suit again, tearing the buttons from their holdings. Baring his body to her, she roughly shoved the material off his shoulders. She growled impatiently, letting her hands roam over his shoulders, his chest, his waist, pushing the homely overalls from his hips, freeing his wonderfully large, delightfully rigid cock.

A tremor of apprehension and anticipation shivered through her at his size. If she were honest she'd have to say she loved every aspect of his size. At five foot, ten inches tall, she towered over most women and it hadn't been easy finding a man who wasn't intimidated by her height. Mac was well over six foot. Probably around six foot four or five and he was brawny, bulky, without an inch of flab anywhere. He made her feel soft, feminine. Who knew feeling small would be so erotic?

She longed to wrap her hand around him. Or better still, to feel the pulsing veins, the throb of the incredibly wide head against her tongue. She wanted to know the feel of him, the taste of him. Eagerly she reached for him and he quickly jerked away from her touch. Covering her mouth with his own, he kissed her, swallowing her whimper of frustration, and she tasted herself, warm and musky. It was so sexy, so extremely arousing. His tongue swept over hers.

"No yet, vixen." He groaned against her lips.

"Yes, now," she begged breathlessly, "I want you inside me, inside my mouth, my pussy. I want you now." Her voice sounded like it was coming from far away. It was low and hoarse with arousal. Pushing him away from her, she let her hand skim down his chest, her nail grazing his nipple causing him to suck in a breath through his teeth.

"Och, aye," he groaned. "Soon, you'll get the chance, Legs. But no yet."

So incredibly hot, his mouth closed over her nipple again, laving it, wrenching a moan from her. They were so sensitive now it was almost painful, but she didn't want him to stop. It was a good pain, a delicious pain. She closed her eyes drinking in the feel of him as she grasped his solid, powerful biceps and relished the feel of his warm taut skin.

The muscles bunched under her hand as he laid her out on the wide plush couch. His eyes traveled her naked body before coming down over her, kissing her shoulders, her collarbone. The slow pulsing arousal that hummed through her began to bloom inside her again, softly swirling, growing outward.

Again she reached for him. She bit her lip as her fingers closed around him. Lightly she began to explore him, moving her fingers up and down his shaft, her thumb brushing over the plum-like crown. Spreading the fluid that flowed from the tip, she frowned. Odd, how it felt different than any she'd ever felt before. Lighter, not as viscous, almost oily and there was more of it. Had he cum already? She started to ask him but his mouth closed hungrily over hers and made her forget all about it.

With a growl, his knee pushed her thighs apart as his hand cupped her sex. The slow burn quickly became an inferno. Draping one leg over the back of the couch she spread her legs for him, giving him better access as his finger lightly grazed the little bundle of nerves at the apex of her pussy, slightly sore from the stimulation it had already received.

Still it greedily plumped at his caress. She moved her hips against his hand and sighed at the tremors that spiraled through her.

"Fuck me, Mac." She met his hot green gaze, begging for more. "Now."

Positioning himself between her thighs, he lifted her arms up over her head and held her wrists against the arm of the couch with one hand. A feral smile curved his sexy mouth at her widening eyes. She knew he could see the excitement, the thrill she felt.

Reaching between them, he took his shaft in his hand and guided the thick head between the sensitive folds of her pussy. Urgently she arched up, making her breasts bounce gently.

"Mmm, now isna that a beautiful sight?" He leaned down to take one incredibly engorged nipple between his teeth before sucking it into his mouth, hard and fast.

The wonderfully thick head of his substantial cock lodged greedily at her opening and she lifted her hips bringing him inside only a fraction.

"Look at me, Ellie." He forced his words through gritted teeth.

She obeyed, opening her eyes as he slowly began to sink into her. She sucked in her breath at the astonishing stretching sensation, the ribbons of hot desire that rippled through her. The pleasure was overwhelming. She felt it radiate from her cunt down her legs, up her abdomen, tightening her nipples, making the very top of her head tingle. Wanting to be filled completely, she narrowed her eyes at him and frowned in concentration as she thrust her hips up for more of him.

His eyes dilated and darkened even more. "Christ, woman. Be still," he snarled at her.

She snarled right back and thrust upward again as best she could, taking him in another inch. God, he felt so good. So incredibly hot. He watched her intently, his eyes gleaming with hunger, his teeth clenching as he tightened his hold on her wrists. A sound somewhere between pleasure and pain, rumbled in Mac's chest as lost control and thrust deeper inside her. Cupping her breast, he gripped the hardened nipple between his finger and thumb, gently tugging and rolling as he watched her reaction. With her head thrown back, she screamed out her pleasure and frustration. The building sensations were driving her mad with desire. With tension clear in his eyes as he struggled for restraint he worked his cock deeper inside her gripping pussy.

"Mmm, you're so tight and wet, Ellie. God, you're so wet. So hot, you're burning me alive, baby."

"Mac," she begged breathlessly. He was ripping her apart and she loved it. More, she wanted much more, she wanted it all.

"What is it, Ellie? D'ye want me to fuck you?" His voice was so wicked, so dark as it rumbled through her, vibrating her.

"Yes, God yes. Fuck me, Mac." She groaned through clenched teeth. Her body shook with desire. Her clit felt huge; like a living thing, it pulsed in time with her rapid heartbeat.

"D'ye want me to fuck you hard, Ellie?" he murmured, tilting his head as he released her hands. With a moan of supreme pleasure he cupped both of her breasts, massaging, molding them.

"Fuck me hard, Mac. Hard and fast," she growled up at him.

Without taking his eyes off her, his hands slid from her breasts, down her body and, grasping her hips, he lifted her and stuffed two small pillows under her ass. Bracing himself, he drove deeper still inside her. He grimaced as he pushed himself inside, deeper into her expanding cunt as it convulsed around his burgeoning shaft. "Goddammit, Elyiana, you're so tight. You feel so fucking good."

It felt as though his erection was expanding even more, impossibly stretching her further. The need, the hunger was a divine and demanding beast that clawed at her, forcing her beyond any pleasure she'd ever imagined and she sobbed with want for more. Slowly he withdrew just a fraction before forcing his thick shaft deeper, and deeper still 'til she was sure he was touching her soul.

His breath came in harsh pants. Wisps of her hair stuck to her sweat-dampened face but she didn't care. Flattening her hand against his trembling stomach she licked her lips and looked up into his eyes. Her fingers traveled down his abdomen to the point where their bodies joined. She trailed a finger around the wide base of his shaft lodged deep inside her and marveled at the amazingly tight ring of her cunt. Thick syrupy arousal soaked her spread lips, his dark auburn curls.

He grasped her hand drawing her cream-soaked finger into his mouth as he licked it clean.

"Mmmm," he groaned. "Sweet."

On a shaky breath she bore down, tightening the walls of her channel, watching his eyes dilate with pleasure. He withdrew halfway then thrust home hard. With a whimper, she arched up, struggling for breath. Meeting his thrust. The heel of his hand pressed down on her lower stomach and she felt his cock rub against the most sensitive spot within her pussy as he withdrew and drove into her again. Increasing his pace, he fucked her faster, the wet sucking sound of his withdrawal and thrust was beyond erotic. Pumping her hips upward, she met each thrust as he slammed into her.

Waves of ecstasy crashed over her with each sweet assault. Each time he withdrew then hammered fast and deep inside her again. Her pussy was so sensitive now. Every thrust filling, expanding, rasping against the muscled walls of her sheath sent sharp shards of sensation radiating through her. Like a lightning flash, her orgasm hit, gripping her in ecstasy.

Again and again he pushed her, drove her until she was sobbing with the unbelievable pleasure. As her last climax gripped her and she shattered screaming his name, her nails bit into his ass, trying to keep him inside her, wanting him deeper still.

Trembling with power-driven aftershocks, she felt him tense as his own orgasm took hold. Looking down into her eyes he plunged into her once more, groaning as his climax surged into her hotly, filling her to overflowing. Lowering himself, he lay across her, his hand smoothing the hair away from her sweat-dampened face.

He frowned down at her for a moment then kissed her like he needed her breath to live. "I want to fuck you, Legs," he growled. "Hard. Fast. Slow and easy. Christ, I don't believe I'll ever get my fill of ye, woman."

Chapter Seven

He couldn't get enough of her. After her climax rocked her body, sending her convulsing around the length of his cock, Mac felt the hunger inside him increasing. He smiled down at her dazed face tightly, seeing the answering spark of pleasure in her eyes.

"Do ye think we're done, lass?" He smoothed his lips over her jawline, fascinated by the taste of her. "Not by a long shot."

Without disengaging, he wrapped his arms around her shoulders, turning effortlessly, distantly amazed that it took no more strength than it did to turn them both until he was on his back, and she was impaled, deeper than before on his surging cock.

"Oh God, you're going to kill me with that thing," she moaned, but it was eroticism rather than pain that filled her voice.

She moved slowly, lifting her hips as she caressed the ultra-sensitive length of his cock with the slick velvet feel of her tight pussy. The walls of her vagina gripped him like a vise and had him baring his teeth in a snarl of pleasure so intense he feared it would take his mind when he finally released inside her.

"There, little love." His body arched as she slid back down the shaft, pressing deeper inside her, feeling her cunt ripple around him with tiny seismic waves of rapture. "Take me as ye please, Legs. Take me all the way."

She took every inch. Her back bowed as he held her hips tightly, her pace increasing with each stroke, making him mad to find his own climax. He moved beneath her, countering his strokes to hers, watching her face as small rivulets of perspiration began to dot it and her eyes became dazed with the sensations building within her.

He could feel it within himself now. His scrotum was tightening, the explosion building in the base of his cock as his spine began to sizzle with the impending eruption.

It was different, but he was too consumed by it to work out the differences. He could feel impulses he had known before, static little waves of building sensation covering his body as he gripped Elyiana's shoulders, dragging her to his chest.

He wanted her to scream for him. Wanted her to know a pleasure unlike anything she had known before. Holding her to him with one arm across her shoulders, he reached along her hips, his fingers trailing through the sensitive crease there as she bucked in his arms.

He drove his cock deep inside the gripping muscles of her pussy as his fingers drew the slick juice that coated the outside to the small, puckered little opening of her anus.

"Wait. Mac," she gasped as he exerted a small amount of pressure to the opening. "Exit only." She struggled in his arms. "Exit only..."

He didn't have to force her to take the width of his finger, he allowed her body to take it instead. The building tension and pleasure whipping inside her had her anal entrance flexing, milking his finger inside as she breathed in roughly, stilling as small, disbelieving whimpers exited her chest.

"My entrance, lass." Just as she was his, he knew. "And best you get used to me there, for soon, verra damned soon, something much larger than my finger will fill ye."

He pressed home as he began to fuck her harder, faster, his finger moving in counterpoint to his cock until he felt his release surging through his cock. Elyiana was screaming in her own climax then, her pussy clamping down on him like the tightest fist as her anal channel spasmed with the climax.

Then he was spilling himself into her, heated, hard jets of seed that filled her milking cunt and had him groaning with the harsh, convulsive spurts that exploded from the head of his cock.

Elyiana collapsed over him, small shudders of the echoing explosion trembling through her body as she slowly relaxed against him. It took her only seconds to drift into sleep while Mac was left frowning at the ceiling above them.

His hand smoothed down her back, feeling the dampness there, but there was none on him. He hadn't broken a sweat, despite the exertion he had put forth. He was breathing heavy from excitement, but not from exertion. He felt he could sleep, but he wasn't tired. And damn it to fucking hell, he was still as hard as he was to start with. Except now, the overriding demand to climax was stilled.

But the climax has been different. Stifled. As though something were missing physically. And he was still hard. Still hot for her.

"Once more, love," he growled roughly, shifting until he had her on her stomach beneath him. One more time.

"Mac." Her voice was weak, but still lusty, still aroused as his hand smoothed over the pert rise of her delicious ass.

He parted the golden globes, running his finger down the shallow crease there.

"Exit only..." she whispered, though not as firmly as she should have, he thought. He could hear the curiosity in her voice, warring with the innocence.

"I told you, lass, my entrance," he whispered, grabbing the bottle of coconut oil from the coffee table. He had eyed it earlier, knowing it would perfect for this little adventure.

"This one last time," he murmured as he tipped the little squirt bottle and squeezed the silky liquid into the crease of her ass.

He watched it run slowly along the path until it met the finger he had pressed just under the little puckered entrance, working it slowly inside the gripping channel.

"Mac..." She trembled before him, but she wasn't refusing him. He felt her muscles clenching, milking his finger, drawing it deeper inside her.

"You'll love it, Legs," he whispered. "Pain and pleasure combined, until you don't know which is uppermost. If you're screaming because the stretching is too much, or screaming because the pleasure is destroying you."

More of the slick oil was worked into the small opening as he added a finger, stretching her, working the delicate little pucker as she moaned around the shallow penetration.

"Feel how good it is, lass," he encouraged her, preparing her gently for him. "Feel how hot and exciting.

A forbidden little pleasure that you'll give to me alone. That's right, isn't it, Ellie? Mine alone."

"Yes," she gasped as he pressed further, pushing his fingers completely inside her, moving them apart, scissoring them back and forth as he worked the muscles apart.

"Oh God, Mac." Her back arched, her fists clenching in the pillowed armrest above her head.

"Good girl," he whispered. "So fucking good. Now comes the best part."

He removed his fingers before applying a thick coating of the oil on his straining cock. By damn, if he didn't lose this hard-on soon he was going to kill himself fucking her. He couldn't get enough.

She was panting for breath as he parted the cheeks of her rear with one hand, and positioned his cock with the other. Gritting his teeth at the pleasure, the eroticism of it, he watched as the thick, mushroomed head tucked into the little entrance.

"Work me in, Legs." He smoothed his hand over her ass a second before he lifted it and let it fall in a sensual little smack on the suntanned flesh.

She jerked, her anus clenching, then opening, working him in the slightest bit.

"Ah, lass, ye like that don't ye?" He smiled in anticipation as her whimpering little moan answered his question. "Let's see how well ye like this."

He raised his hand again, letting it fall more swiftly, striking the pert cheek of her ass hard enough to cause a faint blush to rise beneath the flesh.

"Oh God, Mac..." His cock sank inside her ass a full inch as she pressed back, tightened, opened. Like a tight little fist she milked him.

"Good girl," he smoothed his palm over the reddened flesh, caressing her for a moment, letting his fingers soothe the little sting before he repeated the motion.

Another inch filled her. She was bucking against him, fighting for breath, her body so damp with perspiration that it took very little to make her ass burn from the small slaps. She was writhing beneath him, on fire, her wee little pussy so wet that when his hand moved beneath her to caress the plump lips, she soaked his fingers.

That's how he wanted her. So wet and wild she would suck every last ounce of seed from his balls when he came inside her again.

He applied another small slap, his smile tight, his body so tense he ached now as he pressed deeper, deeper. Sweet heaven, she was taking him, all of him, to the hilt until his scrotum was pressed tight and hard against her soaked cunt. She was slick and hot and destroying any thought he would have had of control. She was twisting, arching back, her ass so slick and tight around him he wondered if he would last more than few seconds before he came inside her.

And he would come inside her. Hard and hot, he'd fill her until there was nothing left to give her.

Gripping her hips to hold her steady now, he drew slowly from the fierce grip she had on him. Watching as his oil-covered cock slowly pulled free until only the thick crest remained. Gritting his teeth he surged slowly back inside her, hearing her throttled scream as he gave her every hard inch in one stroke. Again. He pulled back, surged forward. She bucked beneath him, her cries gasping pleas now as he felt the decadency of the act overpowering her.

Yes, this was how he wanted her. Submissive beneath him, taking all the pleasure he could push inside her and begging for more.

"Harder…Mac, harder…" She was nearly screaming his name now, her little hand tucked between her thighs as she caressed her swollen clit. He knew that little bud was swollen, engorged with the need for release that only he could give her. Only he could give her this, make her burn in this way. By God, he would make certain of it.

At that thought, he lost all semblance of control. Holding her steady he began to fuck her with deeper, harder strokes, growling at the hot grip of her ass as he took her with a pleasure and a passion he knew he had never known before. He watched the possession, the exit and entrance of his erection, the way she bloomed open for him, her flesh reddening, stretching, taking him.

There… His hoarse cry startled him as he felt his scrotum tighten, felt his release burning in his cock.

"Now," he snarled, his hand moving beneath her again, two fingers plunging hard and deep inside her tight pussy as her fingers moved frantically over her clit.

His hips moved faster, harder, his cock surging inside her with hot, furious strokes as he felt her explode around his fingers, his erection, taking him, milking him, throwing him past the edge of sanity.

Words burst from his lips, though he had no clue at the meaning of them. All he knew was the explosive, destroying orgasm that rushed through them both, collapsing them, stealing her last strength, stealing his mind.

Long minutes later he drew back, his cock perhaps not as firm as it had been, but at the very least semi-erect and deflating no further.

What the fuck was going on here?

Slowly, ignoring her grouchy little moans, Mac shifted Elyiana from the couch and carried her into the bedroom to her large bed. She relaxed against her pillow with a little sigh and drifted off again.

Mac ran his hands through his hair, grimacing at the dry feel of it. He should have been sweating like a horse and ready to collapse from fatigue. Then he felt lower, palming his cock and balls as he frowned in confusion. They felt fine. He was still hard when he shouldn't be, and perhaps his scrotum was a shade less heavy than he remembered but he couldn't be certain. Hell, it wasn't as though he weighed the damned things, but perhaps he should have.

It wasn't just that, though. The hair on his body wasn't as thick, not that he was apish, but the hair covering his arms and legs hadn't been as thin as it was now and he could find no explanation for that. But most importantly, his knee wasn't bothering him anymore. He had fractured the damned thing years ago and it still gave him problems when he refused to rest as he should. But it wasn't hurting now, it wasn't even aching.

For a moment, he stilled in shock. That was a memory. He remembered damaging the knee, but not how. He knew it should be aching, knew that he shouldn't have the freedom of movement with it that he was enjoying.

Sighing wearily, he rose from the bed, careful not to awaken the nosey little sprite sleeping beside him. She kept an eagle eye on him while she was awake, making it hard to find time to sort through the problems facing him.

Scratching at his abdomen he moved from the bedroom and padded quickly to the kitchen. He was damned near starving to death, he knew that for certain. Checking her freezer, he pulled out several thick steaks, popped them in them broiler and waited impatiently for them to finish as he prepared his plate and silverware. He wasn't a heavy meat eater, but at this moment he could have eaten the damned things raw if he had to.

Within moments, the auto-broiler finished the two juicy portions of meat and he slid them to the plate before sitting down at the table and devouring them quickly. This hunger confused him more than the other abnormalities he was experiencing. He was eating more than triple his normal amounts.

He cleaned the kitchen, adding his sudden appetite for meat to the list of unreasoned behaviors that he knew wasn't normal. Frustrated by his inability to remember the things he knew he should, Mac left the house and stood beneath the star-studded sky as he attempted to find the answers he needed. Everything seemed in working order. He was eating a hell of a lot more than usual, but it didn't seem to be affecting his weight. High protein foods had become a craving since he awoke in that damned lab four days ago.

All the normal functions were functioning normally, he grunted. Nothing *seemed* wrong, but he knew something definitely *was* wrong. He rarely slept and he was never tired. That one concerned him most of all. The buzzing in his head when he attempted to locate his memories; the feeling of static electricity surging through his body at the oddest times.

And why could he remember trivial information, but nothing important? He could feel the answers there, rolling around in his mind, but he couldn't find the information he needed to pull it all together.

His hand moved to his chest then, running over it curiously. There should be wounds there. Terrible, bloody wounds. The flashes of memory assured him that something had happened there, nearly killed him. But there wasn't even a scar.

He wiped his hands over his face in frustration before sitting down in one of the thickly padded wooden chairs Elyiana kept on the patio. Propping his elbows on his knees he rested his face in his hands and fought the sense of impending doom that gathered within him.

He had come here to protect his woman, but she didn't know who he was. He had memories of her, of taking her, loving her, wanting to wring her damned neck for her innocence alone, but she didn't know him. She hadn't any more idea of him than he had of himself. But the danger was still there, if only he could remember it. And he was terrified that by being here now, he was bringing the threat to her, rather than protecting her from it. And he'd be damned if he wanted to do that. But until he remembered what the danger was, and could determine how to protect her, he didn't know what else to do. Because he couldn't leave her. It would be like ripping out his own soul.

"You've lost your mind, Mac," he told himself bitterly as he stared around the darkness that surrounded him, feeling the primal heat and peace of the land sinking into his mind.

Just as Elyiana had sunk into his soul.

She didn't know him, but he knew her. He couldn't remember her, but he couldn't let go of her. He loved her.

He shook his head at that thought. He shouldn't love her, knew it shouldn't be possible, but he knew he did. And that, he knew, might be the craziest part of it all.

Chapter Eight

Through the haze of sleep she heard Mac curse and turned onto her back. At some point she had kicked her plush comforter off the bed. It was after three a.m. when Mac finally allowed her to sleep and she had been plagued with dark erotic dreams of The MacDougal. Being bound, under his control, his body. Thinking about them now, she moaned and smoothed a hand over her bare stomach. Her limbs were sore as were places she didn't know she had places. But it was a delicious kind of sore, she thought, smiling contently.

Unable to finish the story she'd been working on as she had planned would maybe turn out to be a good thing. Research was crucial to a good story and she believed she had gotten quite a bit accomplished in that area last night. Feeling warm and languid, she'd thought she would have lost her edge. However, her mind was already formulating the scenes. It seemed that she only had more inspiration from which to draw.

"Are ye awake, Legs?" Mac's voice was gruff from sleep deprivation.

Oh hell, she didn't want to open her eyes. Turning onto her side she tried to bury her face into her fluffy pillow with a sigh. There was no going back to sleep now. Already her thoughts were churning with ideas for revamping the story due to the rough and plentiful sex she'd enjoyed, as well as the disturbing dream images that had flashed through her restless mind all night.

"Ellie." He smacked her bottom. "Mmm," she moaned, all for more sex, but not until she had a cup of very hot coffee. With a sigh she rolled onto her back again and pushed her hair out of her face as she stretched and tried to come alive. Carefully she opened one eye. Damn it was bright. Mac's face came into view, his expression grim. Opening the other one she frowned up at him. "What time is it?"

"Nearly noon. I've made coffee." Damn, a headache was budding at her temples. Whimpering, she flattened her palm against his chest and pushed him back as she sat up and rubbed her eyes. Wow, did he always look so good? He felt wonderful, warm and…mmm…naked? No, not naked, he had on Scott's shorts.

"Didn't sleep well, how 'bout you?" she said tilting her head to get a better look at him. The seams of the poor shorts were stressed to the point of breaking and Mac's massive erection was not helping the situation. Blinking at him, she rolled her lips inward. For some reason it struck her as funny to see the giant of a man standing there, his hands on his hips. The tiny shorts weren't even worth the trouble. They hid nothing.

It started as a giggle, then bloomed to a full-fledged laugh. Covering her mouth she looked up and seeing the vexation and affront in Mac's unique green eyes only made it worse.

"Ha' ye gone daft?" he grumbled at her.

"S-Sorry, You just look so cute in your little shorts," she laughed.

"Cute?" A fierce scowl etched lines around his sensuous mouth. His eyes were clear as a cool spring pool and bright with anger. "I'm no a flop-eared pup, woman."

That did it. Elyiana fell back on the bed in a fit of laughter holding her stomach.

"Pull yourself together, Legs, and come into the kitchen. Now." He grunted with finality that only made her laugh harder.

The laughing fit hadn't helped her headache but it was worth it. "Now" he'd said. And she snickered again as she took her time in the bathroom. She ran a hot soapy bath and sighed as it relieved the tension that had built up in her shoulders and neck, the soreness of her muscles. Taking her time, she lathered the natural sponge rubbing over her body, exfoliating and energizing her skin. When she'd finished she leaned back and enjoyed the feel of being cocooned in heat. Letting it permeate her body, loosen the muscles she'd worked out the night before.

Mac's body, his touch was like a drug—one taste and she was addicted. Damn, she never thought she'd come across anything even remotely interesting to her that was more addictive than her morning coffee. Living where she did, she'd even tried cannabis. It had left her feeling like a gluttonous dullard and she'd never bothered with it again. But this was more than interesting. And it wasn't just sex either. She'd had sex at its best as well as so dreadful that there was no way she'd achieve orgasm. But sex with Mac… Wow. That she was afraid she couldn't do without.

But it was even more than the sex that drew her to Mac, something familiar, something she connected with on a deeper level. That thought had been niggling at her for a while now and she couldn't seem to complete the puzzle. The mystic in her told her to be patient, let things just evolve and the truth would eventually reveal itself. But the curious and inquisitive part of her wanted to find and fit the pieces of the puzzle into place. Mac was probably livid by now that she hadn't jumped to obey his command.

A mischievous smile played at her lips as she took a deep breath, held it and slid down into the expansive bath. Completely submerging herself in the soft heat was a ritual she cherished. Staying under as long as she could before emerging rejuvenated. Then she'd use the handheld nozzle to wash her hair and rinse off before getting out and taking on the day. The thumping sound reverberated through the water but before she had time to react large hands grabbed her under her arms and hauled her up.

"Elyiana!" he shouted at her. Pulling her from the tub, his hand swept the hair and suds from her face. She opened her eyes gasping, more in shock than need for air.

"What?" she yelled back at him as he held her soapy, wet body against him. She pushed at his chest to gain freedom but it was a useless endeavor. Cupping her face in his hand, his thumb brushed over her bottom lip.

"You're okay." It was a statement. Confusion clear in his sharp gaze as he assessed her.

Suddenly she became aware of the feel of him, her breasts flattened against his chest, her nipples tightening, his powerful thigh pressing against her wet, naked mound, the impossible rigidity of his erection straining against her stomach. The clench of her vagina, the swelling of her slightly sore, sensitive folds, the liquid arousal that gathered there…it all happened so quickly it took her off guard.

God, she was burning for him. Her blood heated and quickened its pace through her veins. Finally she looked up and met his gaze realizing she wasn't the only one affected by their position.

"I'm fine," she purred, her voice was husky with arousal.

"I thought you were drowning." His emerald eyes narrowed as his hand moved down to cup her ass, sliding her incredibly sensitive pussy over his hard thigh.

She was drowning, but not the way he meant. Her clit began to throb, swell, beg to be touched. Trembling she rubbed against him, moved her hand down his body to free his cock from the ridiculous shorts. "I wasn't drowning," she murmured as she stroked the length of his shaft.

Gazing down at her, Mac stilled. She watched his expression change, his eyes looked through her, past her as if sifting through information. There it was again. She'd caught a glimpse of it yesterday. That lost confusion, frustration, a struggle to grasp some illusive knowledge. Then something inside him shifted and he released her. Quickly.

"Do that again and I'll wring ye wee neck, lass."

"Do what? Take a bath?" Her eyes widened in amazement. "Or stroke your cock?"

"Are ye never serious?" he ground out.

Sadness filled her at the possibility that he had known nothing but seriousness. "The world is a serious place, Mac. Ruthless and sometimes sadistic. You need to cherish the good things, find love and joy in everything you can. Otherwise the horribleness will just consume you."

His jaw tightened, his scowl deepened. "That silly female fluff ideology will get you hurt or killed. Ha' you no sense at all?"

The audacity, the arrogance! Passion swiftly changed to fury as she struggled for her hard won control. "You really are an arse. I've got along just fine without any help from you or any other man for that matter."

"Ha' ye now? It doesna show." Scowling at her, he continued. "You ha' no regard for propriety and take no steps to ensure your own protection. That's more than a little addlebrained, Legs, it's stupid."

She wanted to claw his gorgeous eyes out. Her fists clenched at her sides as she struggled to keep from launching herself at him. "And you are an uptight, socially inept jackass of a man who thinks the world revolves around you and your every word."

"Get dressed, Legs. You and I ha' things to discuss," he snapped angrily then turned to leave. At the door he stopped and turned back. "D'ye think ye have enough sense to dress without killin' yourself?"

"Go away!" she snarled. "I'll be out when I get good and damn ready to come out." She stepped back into her hot bath. "Call me Legs again and I'll hurt you!" *The arsehole.*

The need to scream was overwhelming but she suppressed it, let it spread through her, fuel her resolve to put that pompous self-important gasbag in his place and keep him there. It was his kind that they fought against in the global war. Men and women like him robbed the world of literature, music and art that they deemed indecent, unworthy, without value. Remembering that time, the stories her mother had told her, the things she read about the global war and the frightening years before it, made her throat tighten, her heart clench in her chest.

The loss had been great, it had taken centuries to repair and still things weren't the same. The only print books that still existed were in atmosphere-conditioned cases in her living room. Novels by great writers and not so great writers but still as important, still significant in their own right. Of course her favorites were her romance novels by authors such as Nora Roberts, Sandra Brown, Julie Garwood, Linda Howard, and so many more. Then there were others like Stephen King, Tom Clancy, Maya Angelou. Very few copies remained. Most all had been destroyed in the Obscenity and Indecency Abolition. It was said that they enticed degenerate behavior. Yet her grandmother had saved them, kept them hidden until Elyiana was old enough to realize their importance and cherish them. She did. Oh, how she loved them, she had read them all over and over again.

They were so fragile now she was afraid to take them out. Many she had transcribed onto disc. She read those over and over again, destined to follow in their footsteps. It had been built into her soul, her spirit. From her birth she had passion for life, for the things that humans had the ugly habit of destroying. At the same time she wondered why, how did someone become so cold, so closed off. There had been moments when she looked in Mac's eyes and saw the need there. Well, she could be sympathetic to his pain and she would do her best to help him, but that didn't give him a right to bully her. No, Mac would not intimidate her.

Enough pussyfooting around. If he was right about anything it was that they had things to discuss. Finishing her bath, she hurriedly washed her hair, rinsed off, dried off and quickly pulled on a soft cotton dress. She rubbed at her wet hair, shook her head, tossed her damp hair back from her face and stalked from the room without bothering to brush it. A discussion they would definitely have but contrary to what he foolishly believed, he was not controlling this situation. It was time for him to come clean.

He stood at the freezer seemingly deep in thought when she walked into the kitchen. She crossed her arms and though she could appreciate a nicely shaped ass on a man she refused to let it distract her. Clearing her voice, she waited 'til he gave her his attention. He turned to face her, his irritation faded fast as his gaze skimmed over her, devouring her with his eyes. In response, her pussy throbbed but she pushed the persistent lust aside and frowned at him. "When are you planning on facing the fact that you don't know who the hell you are?"

Chapter Nine

MacDougal Labs, Germany

Amareth stood over the silent form of her brother's body; the machines behind her beeped incessantly. There were no brainwave patterns showing; the machines were keeping his body alive, but the spirit was gone.

She covered her face with her hands, breathing in deeply as she fought for answers, fought to try to figure where Mac had run to. Disoriented as he must have been, he would have surely gone to a place he considered safe. The information inside the electronic brain would be scrambled, but there all the same.

She had personally checked all his properties, all the little out of the way haunts he had retreated to before, as well as a few she felt he would have never returned to. He wasn't there.

The MacDougal security force was searching high and low for the missing android, unaware they were actually searching for their boss, but he hadn't been seen. The jet glider was nowhere on the Global Positioning Satellite. It was as though he had disappeared off the face of the Earth.

"This isn't helping, Amareth." Behind her, Tael's voice chastised her for her vigil over Mac's body. "This isn't helping him."

She closed her eyes briefly. She could see him, tall and dark, his shaggy black hair falling to his collar, his intense gray eyes darkening with a hunger that never failed to tempt them both. A hunger she knew she could never fulfill, not ever again. The risks were too great.

She shook her head fiercely. "I'll find him. I've never failed Mac. I won't begin now."

But she had. She had failed him when she had forced the transference of his life force into a unit unprepared for it. God, what had she done?

"I didn't say you were failing him," Tael gritted out. "I said, all this isn't helping anything. You're sitting there beating yourself up over the decision you made when both of us know you had no choice at the time. It was a viable risk."

"One that failed." She kept her voice cold, hard, but inside she could feel the tears begging to be free. "I'm no closer to finding the mole or to understanding what happened. His personal bodyguards as well as the assailants are dead and the reporters are eating me alive. They know something's wrong. They're like vultures, scenting death."

She tightened the grip she had taken on her brother's hand. She had never been without Mac in her life. He had always been there for advice, for guidance.

She ran her fingers wearily through her loose hair, searching for answers. There had to be something, somewhere, but where? She knew the code he used for his personal journal, and there had been nothing there to indicate where he had gone.

A smile almost touched her lips. He was furious at the newly emerging novelist, Elyiana Richards. He had found the hidden stash of books Amareth had been reading, and curious, he had opened the files and checked them out himself.

Fondly, she thought of the harsh words he had written in his journal. A woman who needed her rosy glasses jerked aside so she could see how the world really was, he had written. Soft, filled with fantasy and a babe in the woods. A woman that wouldn't know a real man if he was fucking her.

But there was no answer to where he had flown.

"The reporters always react this way to his disappearances," Tael snarled. He always snarled at her. "The company isn't suffering, and everyone who knows Mac or has any experience with him thinks nothing of it. We'll scrape by on this one and soon Mac will be at the helm again."

Mac was going to kill her. She couldn't ease the panicked feeling in her stomach that warned her that a storm was brewing. He hadn't known about the physical design of the sexual android that the development arm of the company was working on. In her anger at him, her arrogant belief that she was getting one over on him, Amareth had ordered the design in his likeness, as he had been years ago. Before they had lost their parents through an act of violence. Before Mac had turned hard, cold.

As Tael moved around the medical bed, she composed her expression, her eyes. She couldn't allow him to see her weakness, her fears.

She looked up at him, her heart clenching at the sight of his perfect features and dark good looks. Tael was tall, as were all of those in the MacDougal line, broad and strong, a force to be reckoned with. And he was honorable, as arrogant and trustworthy as Mac himself.

"How do you expect this android to work?" he finally asked her. "Is there anything we could use to help us find it?"

Amareth shook her head bitterly. "We were thorough in the design. Once it was programmed with the human responses—sense of taste, smell, feel, sight and hearing—it became self-sufficient. The internal batteries are fueled from food. High protein foods for the most part are broken down similar to the manner a human body uses. The reason the sexual units haven't worked before was because you could tell they were sexual units. Our test subjects wanted something they could convince themselves was real, while still retaining control.

"The units were programmed to simulate actual human responses. They weren't meant for what happened." Frustration edged her voice until she gained control of it. "I don't understand this, Tael, none of the other models sucked the very spirit out of the men we programmed them with. I can't figure out how it happened."

She had run every test imaginable, had gone over that particular droid's programming with a fine-toothed comb. All the fail-safes had failed. Mac had somehow overridden every security control in place on the model. It wasn't possible, yet it had happened.

"What would have happened if the transference had failed?" he asked her then.

She sighed heavily. "The body would have died. Somehow, when he moved into the unit's housing, his body didn't experience the rejection most go through when bodily functions and brain patterns are slowed down. It's as though the human body is now computerized, allowing us to sustain it through the machines, where before, in all cases, the body has rejected the lack of stimulation and in many cases died within hours."

"He's alive then, that's all that matters. When he's found, can you effect another transfer?"

The million-dollar question.

"I think so," she said cautiously. "I believe this happened because Mac knew he was dying. His will is so strong. His determination pure steel. If he wants to go back, then he will."

Nothing else was said. Tael continued to watch her with that manner he had, as though he was trying to see deeper into her than she wanted anyone to delve.

She gave her brother's hand a final squeeze before she rose to her feet, jerking her black synthetic leather jacket from the back of the chair and shrugging it to cover the weapon holster she wore at her side, before leaving the room.

"I have to get back to headquarters," she said crisply. "I have one of the techs working on a more sensitive GPS locator. He swears that even damaged or crashed it should pinpoint the location of the jet glider. I have to nudge him a bit and see if he can't get it going sooner than expected."

"Bully him you mean?" Tael snapped then, back to his ever-present snarling self.

She glanced at him in surprise. "Not unless he needs bullying." She shrugged carefully. "Personally, I thought I should try sweet persuasion first."

She gave him a cold, toothy smile.

His brows snapped into an instant frown.

"You wouldn't know sweet persuasion if it fucked you," he informed her snidely. "You're probably terrifying the kid into working faster. That won't get the job done, Amareth."

She stilled the flash of hurt that his words caused. He made her sound mean, cruel. She wasn't. Sometimes she had to pretend to be, but it often hurt her more than she could ever let Tael see.

Rather than snapping back with a waspish reply, she lifted her brow mockingly instead.

"I'll be certain to take your complaints to Mac when he returns," she told him as though they didn't really matter.

"Mac would commend you," he continued the verbal assault as Amareth fought to hold onto her control. "You're the perfect little soldier. Cold and hard, just as he wanted you to be."

He was close to the fight he was obviously looking for.

"Cold enough that you can't hurt me," she told him mockingly instead. "Hard enough to remind you that even if I can't kick your arse myself, I can make you hurt. Remember that Tael, before you decide to rake me over the coals over something you have no clue what you're talking about."

She turned to leave the room, to escape the tightening of her throat as she stared into the dark depths of his eyes. There was more there than she wanted to see, and she would be damned if she wanted to ache for something else she couldn't have.

"When are you going to be a woman, Amareth, instead of Mac's arse kicker?" He finally asked her, his voice rough-edged, brewing with anger as she stopped at the door.

"I don't know, Tael," she finally answered coldly, turning back to stare at him condescendingly. "Maybe about the same time you finally get the balls to admit you're too fucking scared of Mac to go after what you really want. When you can do that, then we can discuss my shortcomings."

Before he could respond, before the fury that flashed in his eyes erupted, Amareth escaped the lab and the heat that sizzled through her body each time she watched those incredible dark blue eyes fire with his rage, or his passion.

He was tempting. Too tempting for her own peace of mind right now. She didn't have time to fight with him to torture herself with what was never going to be. She had to find her brother, and that meant thinking like Mac. Problem was, she had come to the conclusion years before that Mac was just an anomaly. There was no thinking like him, there was no understanding him. He just was…

Chapter Ten

"When are you planning on facing the fact that you don't know who the hell you are?"

Mac stilled. He held her gaze, seeing her complete belief in the conclusion she had come to. Damn her, she was smarter than he had given her credit for. He wasn't a lad still wet behind the ears, he knew how to handle himself, and he knew he had given her nothing to betray the confusion in his own mind. Or at least, he hadn't though he had. At this point, he couldn't really be certain.

The jumbled mass of memories was still too confusing, too scattered in his own mind to make sense. There one minute, gone the next, it was damned frustrating as hell to deal with.

"I've faced it." There was no sense in lying about it. Keeping it from her was grating on him anyway. If anyone had a need to know, it was Elyiana, though why he wasn't certain other than the fact that the sense of danger he had felt before was only growing stronger.

There were too many flashes of memories of blood, pain…death. It made no sense, and attempting to make sense of it only caused more confusion. He was locked within his own mind, at the mercy of time to reveal the truth. But he trusted his Ellie, his Legs. Somehow he knew there would be no betrayal from her.

He knew there was something different about her. Something softer, yet stronger than any other woman he had known. He couldn't remember the other women, but his sense of it was there.

She stared back at him, those incredible violet eyes of hers wary, intent as she watched him.

"So why didn't you tell me?" she asked him then, more than a little confused, her frown deepening. "We could have been searching for information, trying to locate your family."

That was exactly what he didn't want. He could feel the danger rising now, an imperative demand that he not allow her to go searching for anything.

"No." He shook his head in denial, moving quickly to her as she stood her ground, preparing to argue. "Listen to me, Legs, and listen well. I dinna know what happened to me, or why I canna remember but I know alerting anyone to the fact that I'm still alive isna' a good idea right now."

He wanted to shake his head at the distant echo of pain in his chest, the broken images of blood and pain that assaulted the few hours he had managed to sleep. He should be dead, he knew that. Just as he knew that until he remembered exactly what had happened, he was more afraid of the danger he would place her in, than the danger to himself.

She was watching him too closely now, too intently. What was it about her eyes? About her? It was as though she could see into his soul, and frankly, the thought of that terrified him even as it soothed some wild, untamed part of his soul that he was unaware existed until now.

He could almost see her mind working now, though what she was thinking he had no clue, and he very much suspected he didn't want to know.

"Amnesia," she said carefully. "They can treat that now, Mac."

Denial raged through him. He had already considered that option. His mind was filled with a vast array of information that made no sense, and among it was the scientific treatment for amnesia. The brain was an amazing living computer; you just had to know how to access it properly.

"It will return." He finally shrugged, rubbing at his chin thoughtfully. "Strangely, I thought *you* should know who I am. It's why I came here. I know you; at least I feel I do. But the things I know make no sense."

He shook his head. He couldn't get the image of fucking her deep and slow on a boardroom table out of his mind. Laying her back on it, spreading her legs wide as he sat in the comfort of one of the deeply upholstered chairs as his mouth made a sensual meal out of the syrupy sweetness he found there. Hearing her cries, her pleas that he take her, the music of her passion was destruction. But he was getting a feeling she didn't have those memories.

"But Mac, how could I know you?" She shook her head in confusion. "I've never met you."

"You dinna know me at all?" he finally asked her with a sense of resignation.

It hurt. He didn't want to admit it, but something pricked at his already ragged emotions at the knowledge that she truly didn't know him. Until now, he had held out hope, a small flicker of it, that they had at least met, that perhaps for some reason, she just hadn't wanted to admit to whatever had been between them. A false hope, and he had known it even before now.

He watched as she licked her lips nervously, her pink little tongue dampening the pouty curves he was dying to taste.

"You look familiar," she finally admitted as she flushed a delicate pink.

Interesting. The color in her cheeks and the wry amusement mixed with passion in her eyes piqued his curiosity. And his jealousy.

"How?" He stepped closer, his faulty memory not nearly as imperative as learning why she was heating so damned fast. He could almost smell her pussy creaming.

She shrugged, clearing her throat.

"That doesn't matter. What matters is finding out who you are." She would have turned away from him, he could see the retreat in her eyes and he wasn't having it. He had messed up the night before and he knew it. He wouldn't make that mistake today. If he didn't sate the lust driving him insane first, then he would never be able to figure out the problem in his mind.

"Och, what matters is finding out how hot ye can burn, lass,"

Mac watched her eyes darken, watched the blush of arousal that instantly stained her cheeks and had to grit his teeth to hold onto the control that he knew he had never had a problem exercising before.

"Wait," she responded breathlessly as his lips neared hers. "This isn't the time for this, Mac. We have to find out—"

He didn't give her time to complete what she would have said. Nothing was more important than tasting her, than feeling her kiss again and the fire that raged through his system each time he touched her. It was paradise. It was unlike anything he had ever known.

His lips covered her. The soft curves cushioned against him, opening for him as his tongue licked at them. The taste of her set fire to his loins, had him groaning with the need to fill her now, hard and fast. But he wanted to savor her as well. He wanted to experience every little moan, every tensing of her body and catlike flexing of her muscles.

His hands moved to her buttocks, the smooth curves tempting him to trace and memorize every line. Instead, he fisted his fingers in the fabric covering them and began to draw it along her thighs as his lips moved to the graceful arch of her throat.

"This is insane," she protested weakly, but her hands were kneading at his bare shoulders, her little nails scratching erotically at his skin and sending electrical trills of pleasure shooting through his body.

He could feel his nerve endings sizzling with sensation. Little flares of heat that threw him off balance, made him eager to intensify them to find out how high and hot they could burn together.

He knew he should be more concerned with learning who he was, what had happened. It wasn't like him he sensed, to take physical pleasure over the need for answers. But he was consumed with her. Obsessed with her. The images of her in his mind, taking her in so many different ways, knowing her as he had never known another, rocked through his brain, his body.

"Aye, insanity," he agreed as the material of her dress cleared her thighs, giving him access to bare, warm flesh. "And one I eagerly embrace."

Her hands were roving over his shoulders now, his upper back, stroking the fires in him hotter than ever. Elyiana was hotter than any flame he had ever experienced. The fingers of one hand delved between her smooth buttocks, finding the creamy slick essence of her internal fires.

"Ach, lass, you're wet and hot for me. Just as ye should be." He lifted her, forcing her thighs to open, to clasp his hips as he ground her pussy against the hard ridge of his cock.

Her gasp of pleasure was like fuel thrown on his overheated senses, his engorged erection. His teeth scraped her neck, nipping at it as he grimaced with the riotous pleasure.

"Mac, this is killing me," she cried out her own desperation as her fingers pushed at the snug material that stretched over his hips. "Do something."

He growled at her demand, grinding her more firmly against his swollen length. Oh, he had intentions of doing something to her. More things than she could imagine.

She writhed against him, stroking his lust higher, making him nearly as insane as she accused him of being. He'd had enough of it. He was starved for her taste, her touch. With a fierce growl he turned, propping her sweetly curved rear on the counter as he pushed her thighs wide.

Her excited mewls were driving him past the edge of reason. He ripped at the shorts tightening over his straining cock as he lowered his head, pressing her back until he could reach the glistening, cream-soaked curves of her cunt.

He didn't go for preliminaries this time. No tentative licks or gently touches, he buried his mouth in the soaked slit, his tongue plunging forcefully inside the creamy center as he devoured her.

He heard her screaming his name, felt her pussy convulse but gave her no mercy. His tongue fucked into her hard and fast, drawing more and more of the silky syrup from her and reveling in the taste of her. Exotic, erotic, a temptation that set his blood pressure rising as she climaxed to his oral ministrations.

"Mac, fuck me," she cried out even as the sweet essence of her release was captured by his tongue. "Now, Mac. Fuck me now."

How could he deny her? Her passion was so sweetly given, so pure, tempting. He rose swiftly to his feet, watching her through narrowed eyes as he lodged the head of his erection at the snug portal of her pussy.

"This is mine." His hands clenched at her hips in demand. "Do you understand me, Ellie? Mine. No others."

She stared back at him, her dark eyes glittering with her own hunger as she stared back at him.

"Yours, Mac," she swore then. "As long as you're mine, I'm yours."

It was a bargain well met.

"Yours," he whispered, pressing forward, his teeth gritting at the hot, snug clasp that began to glove him. "Always love, always yours..."

Something in his soul splintered, fragmented. He had never given himself in such a way to another and he knew it. He knew it, but it didn't matter, not anymore. He had been born for this woman, for this moment.

He surged inside her, hard and deep, forcing his cock past the restricting muscles as she arched to him, milking him in, her moans pushing him to take her harder, faster, deeper.

He worked the stiff length deeper into the slick channel, gritting his teeth at the feel of her. She was like silk, like velvet. Hot and liquid, but tighter than a fist. The conflicting sensations were ripping him apart.

"Take me, baby," he urged her roughly as the tight clasp held him back, forcing him to work his flesh in slowly, inch by inch. "Relax, sweetheart, let me in."

He stared into her eyes, narrowing his own as she smiled back with a sultry wickedness that had his cock hardening further, though he wouldn't have thought it possible.

"Make me," she whispered breathlessly, tightening further, her vaginal muscles clamping down on him as he fought the release welling in his scrotum.

"Lass, you're gonna regret this." His hands tightened on her hips as he fought for control. "I dinna want to hurt ya."

Her hands stroked over his chest before she bent her fingers, allowing her nails to rasp his skin with an edge of pain.

"Take me, Mac," she whispered then, her oddly colored hair framing her face, her deep violet eyes, wanton and wicked. "Take me like you mean it…"

Like he meant it? God above only knew how much he meant it. His hands tightened further on her hips, holding her steady as he pulled back, watching her, unwilling to go past the limits of painful pleasure. He paused, watching as she licked her lips, her sultry, tempting gaze too much for a man to resist.

With a shattered groan he plunged home, forging ahead until every thick inch of his cock was buried in the furnace of her ever tightening pussy.

She screamed, her face flushing further, neck arching as she gave to him. Control was now a thing of the past. There was none, no need for it. Holding her close he began to fuck her with every primitive urge he had ever kept locked inside his mind. His mouth lowered to her neck, his lips covering a small spot and suckling it in. He wanted to mark her, fuck her until insanity took them both, and possess her heart as surely as she possessed his.

He hammered inside her, his breathing rasping from his chest as he felt her gripping him, flexing, then exploding around him in a rush of heat and flames that triggered his own climax and had him crying out against her damp neck as he began to pump every ounce of his seed inside her. And still it wasn't enough. Still he needed more…

He lifted her, his hands pressing into the rounded globes of her delectable ass, and carried her quickly to the living room. To the couch. He wasn't nearly finished with her. The hunger inside him felt insatiable, almost…nearly…inhuman.

Chapter Eleven

Everything faded but the feel of his shaft forcing her open. Mac rammed into her, his balls slapping at her swollen clit, his thumb firmly, slowly rubbing the tender flesh that separated her vagina from her rear channel. She cried out as she felt herself soar toward another orgasm. She clutched back of the couch she bowed her back, rocking against him, meeting each savage thrust.

"That's good, Christ, woman, yes," Mac hissed, lightly slapping her ass.

Caught in the grip of a maelstrom of sensation, Elyiana momentarily forgot to breathe and her nails dug into the fabric of the couch. "God yes, Mac. Again!" she demanded.

Withdrawing his thumb, he inserted instead one long finger, then, slowly working in another, he slapped her ass again. The bite of pain only intensified the pleasure. Her body trembled as the violent orgasm shook her to the core. She screamed his name, sobbing with every swell, every wave that broke over her, taking her breath and her sanity with it.

Gripping her hips, he hammered harder and harder. One orgasm blended into another and all she could do was hold on, ride out the storm. His roar of release shuddered through her as his fingers bit into her flesh, filling her with his white-hot seed. Still pulsing, she trembled as he wrapped his big arms around her and pulled her down onto his lap.

She curled into him her breath still coming in harsh pants, his rigid cock still lodged inside her. How could he still be hard? They'd fucked four times. Four! "Mac?" she murmured snuggling against him, letting her cheek rub against his chest.

"Hmm?" His reply was distant, deep in thought.

"I want you to know that it's not that I don't admire your prowess and your magnificent potency. But, I think my poor pussy needs time to recover." Inside her, his cock jerked and she winced at the pleasure/pain that flooded her. "Or…maybe not." She whimpered.

The soft rumble of his chuckle felt good against her cheek, as did the tightening of his arms around her. The walls were down, if only for this moment, they were down enough that he laughed. She could get way too used to this. Although the sex just might kill her. Just how much pleasure could a body take before it gave up? A smile curved her lips and she closed her eyes. Perhaps they would find out. She prided herself on doing thorough research.

"I'm no a sadist, love. I'll no push ye too hard." He kissed the top of her head and moaned as she wiggled on his lap. "But a man has his limits. Maybe we should get up before I forget that ye have limits of your own."

"I think maybe I detect a dare. Just maybe we should go at it like minks and see which of us gives out first." Raising her head, she bit at his muscled neck as she threaded her fingers through his wonderful hair.

He caught her arms and held on to them. "I dinna think that would be a wise challenge to make, Legs." The humor left his voice and a shiver of apprehension snaking through her.

"Oh! So you think me weak do ye?" she asked, mocking his thick brogue in an attempt to chase away the dark mood that had come over him.

Pulling her away from him, he held her gaze. "No. Ah don't." he said firmly. "No' at all, Elyiana."

For the longest time she studied his eyes, trying to reach deeper until his lids lowered and he captured her mouth in a quick kiss. "Get dressed, Legs. We can continue the erotic Olympics after you've ha' time to recover a wee bit."

Kissing him again, she pulled away and lifted herself from his rigid shaft with a grimace. Regardless of her bravado, he was right. She needed time to recover. "Chicken," she teased. "I'm all sweaty. Let's grab a quick shower."

"Right behind you, Legs." He stood and patted her ass.

Giving him a smirk, she tossed her head as she turned and walked away. All at once it dawned on her that he wasn't the least bit sweaty. That mane of thick hair was just as dry and fluffy as when they started their sex marathon. It wasn't as if he didn't get hot. She'd felt his skin heat, quite a bit. And his ejaculation was different too, not just warm, almost hot and so silky smooth inside her. Soothing. Well maybe it was just the way of him, she considered. Maybe he just didn't sweat a lot. She'd had several different men but not a vast array. Maybe his cum was just different.

Inside the spacious shower stall, hot water jets pelting their bodies gently, they soaped each other with thick fragrant lather. Mac took the sponge from her. "Turn around," he commanded.

Had she not relished the idea of having her back washed she would have rebelled. Instead she sighed as he took his time caressing her, washing away the tension along with the sweat. Between the hot shower and the slow gentle massage, Elyiana's body felt sated and relaxed. Fisting his wet hair in her hand she pulled his head down to her, and took his bottom lip gently between her teeth, letting her tongue trace over it. Teasing him with quick lusty kisses and licks, she let go of his hair and ran her fingertips down the hard muscles of his shoulders and chest.

With a groan he gripped her waist and jerked her against him, his head tilting to give him better access to her mouth, but she pulled away. "No," she whispered. "My turn."

"Mmm, aye" he murmured as her lips closed around his nipple.

Enjoying her exploration she took her time, letting her mouth move down his body. Indulging in the taste of him, learning the feel of him on her tongue. With her hands on his hips she knelt before him. Proudly, his cock stood impossibly erect, jutting toward her in anticipation. She lifted her eyes slowly to meet his gaze. She loved the way he watched her as she licked the water from the tip of his cock.

Heavy lidded, his lips parted, his hand smoothed her hair back from her face. Her heart thudded against her chest as her fingers closed around the base of his rigid shaft. Again she licked at the tiny opening then the seam underneath. Holding his gaze she traced the flared ridge of the thick head with her tongue and her lips nipped at the velvety tip. Slowly her hand moved up and down the rigid shaft.

Drawing a breath in through his teeth, his fingers speared into her hair as she opened her lips over the broad head, drawing him in. With her free hand, she lightly cupped his balls; gently her fingertips massaged the tender spot behind them.

"Christ, Ellie," he hissed as she took him deeper, sucking, stroking him with firm caresses of her tongue, her fingers. So hot, so thick and strong. She took him, swallowing as he began to thrust. Closing her eyes she drew on him; her head bobbed faster as he began earnestly fucking her mouth.

"God yes, suck me harder." His balls tightened, drawing upward. Eager to obey she sucked him greedily. It wouldn't surprise her if she came with him; her vagina tightened violently at his demand, flooding her pussy with her juices. The thick ridge running along the bottom of his shaft pulsed against her tongue and she moaned, vibrating around him. Lost in the feel of him, in the pleasure she gave him, he gave her.

"Ellie," he warned, his voice hoarse with desire.

No, she didn't want him to pull away now; she wanted to taste his pleasure. Clinging to him, she took him over the edge. With a roar, his head fell back; he exploded. Hot jets of his seed pumped into her mouth. Holding onto him, she took all he gave her, licking the very last drop before he lifted her.

Oddly his cum wasn't bitter, nor was it all that salty as had been her experience on the few occasions she had done this before. On the contrary, it was a bit sweet, and smooth. But then Mac wasn't at all like any other man. Shrugging it off, she let him pull her up into his arms to kiss her thoroughly. His body stilled as his tongue swept the interior of her mouth.

Pulling away she looked up, meeting his gaze. Though he was looking at her it was obvious that his mind was somewhere else. "Mac? Is something wrong?"

"No." His frown faded into that non-expression he wore most of the time. "No, Legs, everything's fine."

"Sure?" she asked narrowing her eyes. Everything had happened so fast, she shouldn't expect him to open to her. But she did. She hated the way he could close himself off. Shut her out in an instant, without any warning.

"Absolutely," he said. "Let's get out of this box before we turn into wrinkly prunes."

Things had progressed quickly, though. In time, she told herself, shrugging off her discomfort. What would be perfect now, she thought, stepping out of the stall, is to curl up under her thick fluffy comforter and take a nap. But there was too much to do if she was going to help Mac get some answers. It was obviously weighing heavily on his mind. She could only imagine how disconcerted he must feel.

Watching him dry off, she shook her head. He seemed even more energetic than before. It was a miracle, a man who didn't collapse into a snoring heap after sex. If it weren't for that tiny little dictatorial flaw of his, the man would be perfect.

"I have to make a pot of coffee. I'm approaching desperation here." She yawned.

Standing in the middle of her bedroom completely naked, his hands on his hips, his magnificent cock still primed and at the ready, Mac glanced at her, irritation clear in his expression. Oddly, it lightened her mood. Irritation was an emotion. Any emotion was better than none. "You go ahead and get online, I'll make the coffee. And hunt up something to eat."

Watching him fume as he tried to decide what to do about his lack of apparel, Elyiana bit her lip to keep from grinning. "You can wear my nightshirt. It will be a bit tight but…"

Holding up a hand to stop her, he scowled. "I dinna think so."

"So go naked." She shrugged, pulling the sundress over her head and letting the soft material glide down over her body. "I'm not expecting anyone." She let her gaze travel his body appreciatively and slowly lifted a brow. "I surely don't mind."

He narrowed his eyes. "It would be best if we had a barrier between us, Legs. At least for a while."

He turned to go find Scott's discarded shorts she assumed. Sighing deeply, she tilted her head as she watched him walk away. It should be illegal to have an ass so perfectly sculpted.

"And ye best put some panties on too, love, and no' those wee ones, either," he shouted at her from the kitchen.

With a smirk, she pulled on her clean cotton panties. These were designed for comfort alone. Maybe that would cool his libido for a while. Didn't do a damn thing to help hers, though. Even walking to her desk in the living room was a chore. The flesh between her thighs was still swollen, achy and any friction at all seemed to be stimulating. Sighing again, she lowered herself into the thickly cushioned desk chair, tucked a leg under her and booted up.

Finding the site she wanted wasn't hard and she'd just started filling out the form. "Mac. Do you have any distinguishing marks, piercings or tattoos? I sure as hell didn't see any but…"

"No, stop." He came rushing in from the kitchen. "That will be traceable, Ellie."

"Crap." She frowned at the computer. "You're right."

"We'll ha' to search all the missing persons files," he said, going back to what he was doing.

"That's going to take forever, Mac." This was only going to complicate things more.

"Oh aye. But we ha' no other choice in the matter." Resigned, Mac's voice was quiet but firm.

She reached for the mug he offered just as the communicator beeped, signaling an incoming call. Intently watching her from behind her desk, he shook his head and she gave him a "well, duh" look as she clicked to receive the transmission. Scott's smiling face filled the screen.

"G'day, beautiful. Thought I'd look in on you, see how you're doing."

Scott always made her smile. "Hey, babe. I'm so glad you called. I'm tied up here with this new story and I need you to do me a favor."

"Anything, love, you know that." He winked at her and she couldn't help but grin.

It slipped a bit when she glanced up at Mac. His eyes glittered with anger, his lips pressed together and that sexy muscle in his jaw was flexing. Damn, if it didn't drive her crazy when he got mad. Shifting in her chair, she cleared her throat. "I have a friend staying with me and he's needing a few things, some clothes, shoes…"

"A friend? Do I know him?" Scott asked as the scowl on Mac's face deepened.

"No, but he's a great guy. No worries!" Her laugh lacked humor and she would be willing to bet her smile was just a bit tight. All the testosterone was giving her a headache. Why all of a sudden was she plagued with protective male types who wanted to treat her like some fragile flower? Sheesh! "So be a love and pick up the clothes for me. Oh and some fresh fruit, milk, rice..." Mac distracted her and mouthed the word "meat". She frowned at him but he just narrowed his eyes and nodded. Turning back to the screen she added "...and lots of red meat."

"Red meat? You've never been a big meat eater, El. Don't you still have some of that fresh fish we caught last month?"

"Yes, Scott, but I'd like some steaks a couple of nice roasts and maybe a chicken...or two," she added glaring back at Mac.

Scott narrowed his eyes at her. "Are ya sure you're all right, love?" Then his eyes widened as something horrendous dawned on him and Elyiana braced herself. "You're not pregnant are you?"

"Ah, don't be a dunderhead! You know I've been inoculated," she barked at him as a smile tugged at the corner of her mouth. Whether it was because of Scott's expression or the growl that came from Mac's direction as he began to pace, she saw the wisdom in completing the call. Quickly, she gave Scott the sizes Mac needed, said goodbye and disconnected. Innocent-eyed as she could possibly be, Elyiana sat back in her chair and watched Mac from over her mug as she sipped from it. "When you're done pacing like a caged lion, we'll get busy."

Mac seemed at odds with his emotions. As though he didn't know what to do with them, where they fit in. He stopped and looked down with such fierceness she half expected him to bare his teeth and hiss. Lifting a brow, she waited for him to go on a tirade. Fascinated, she watched him struggle. He opened his mouth then closed it again, "Let's just get this done," he grumbled finally.

A slow smile spread across her face. "What a great idea. Wish I'd thought of that."

Chapter Twelve

"Where the hell are you, Mac?" Amareth stood in the middle of her brother's office, turning in a slow circle, her hands propped on her hips as she stared around the ultra-neat space he kept.

There wasn't so much as a piece of paper out of place. The room, despite being the one place Mac virtually lived in, appeared as sterile and well-kept as any lab. The few personal touches he had added were on his desk. A few framed images of her and Jaime. One of their parents.

She walked over to the antique oak wood desk, staring down at the holographic display of her parents. James MacDougal and his wife, Claire, had been a force to be reckoned with during the final stages of Global Economic and Social Reconstruction that had come about after the wars. The Coalition had been more than a century in progress at that time, but her parents, along with many of the other more influential families, had thrown in their fortunes and their vast knowledge to complete the process.

In doing so, they had made enemies. Terrible, evil enemies. Enemies that had eventually murdered them and nearly took their children with them. Mac had witnessed the brutal slaying, lived with his own sense of helplessness in his attempts to save his parents, and had been molded by the discovery that it had been family who had revealed the hidden location the MacDougal and McLeod families were hidden at during that time.

It was a trusted friend who had betrayed Mac this time as well.

Lawrence MacGillan had been a childhood friend to both her and Mac. For years he had been a trusted employee, privy to many of the MacDougal security codes and sensitive company information. Learning he had betrayed them had been a bitter pill to swallow. Having him attempt to kill her when she slapped the evidence down on his office desk had been shocking.

Sighing wearily, she sat down in the synthetic leather comfort of her brother's chair and stared at her hands. There was no blood on them, but they should have been stained to the bone. She had killed, not just Lawrence who had betrayed Mac's whereabouts to his enemies, but she had killed others as well.

Amareth had witnessed the terrifying murder of her parents along with her brother; she had seen his determination, the near superhuman effort he had made to save her and their younger brother.

She had sworn that night that she would never betray Mac, never let him down. She would be his right hand, she would make certain she did everything better, brighter, faster than anyone else, to repay him. To show him her dedication in return for her life. And to protect him. Because no matter the shield he placed between him and the world, it had been she, Amareth who held him after the frantic escape, his body raging with fever from his wounds, and swore to her loyalty to him.

"Dinna betray me, Am," he had demanded bleakly as his body shuddered with racking chills. "Swear to me, Am. Swear ye'll never betray me."

And she hadn't. Not ever. Until now. It was her fault he was now helpless, in danger. Where the fuck could he be?

Once again she keyed his personal code to his daily journal. She hadn't found anything in there the other hundred times she had checked, but she kept hoping. There was nothing else that could hold the answers.

As the holographic image of the computer screen blinked into existence, she frowned at the red flag that blinked in the day's date. That hadn't been there before. A reminder of some sort that she hadn't seen in the log. She hit the appropriate key on the corresponding board that came up on the desktop and watched curiously.

The Laird's Downfall…publication date July 12, 2375. Synopsis, Douglas MacRoberts learns there's more to his shy assistant than meets the eye.

As a government spy, Celine is working as the Scots Laird's assistant to investigate claims that Douglas has betrayed his planet and his people. Is Douglas her enemy, or the lover who has sworn his devotion? And if it's not him who is suddenly threatening her life, then who else could it be?

Personal note: Reminder to fly to Australia and show Ms. Richards exactly how a Scots Laird takes vengeance. That the damned little upstart should dare to finally cross the line and insert both physical and character traits of myself is too much. She needs a decent fucking to show her that sex is more than candy and roses and men are a damned sight more dangerous than the pansy-assed little morons she uses as heroes. I've grown tired of her nits and picks, deliberately placed within her novels after my first objection to the fluff her publisher chooses to place in the hands of our women. The woman has no sense of decorum, nor of the fairytales she's convincing women are truth. But it's time she finds out. Because this Scots Laird has had enough…

Amareth was tempted to laugh. Mac had been in a rampage for more than a year over Elyiana Richards, the rapidly rising star of the reemerging fiction genre called erotic romance. Amareth herself devoured the books, wishing for a world such as the writer described, escaping from the reality of her existence into one where she could let her dreams pour forth and let the adventures the author weaved fill her soul.

Mac had been outraged to learn his sister read what he called "destructive trash". And swore that at first opportunity he was heading to Australia to…

She sat up straight, her eyes widening. Oh God, it was right there in front of her eyes all this time, and she hadn't seen it. One of her last conversations with Mac had been his furious claim that if he were a better man he would just shut the damned publisher down. He did after all own controlling interest in it. He had been incensed, swearing that Elyiana Richards was using *him* as a basis for her heroes.

Amareth had laughed and denied it, but to be honest, she had begun suspecting that herself in the past year. It was well-known to a very select few that Mac had managed to spark the writer's temper with his first vitriolic email to her publisher. Richards had personally written him then, informing him that he was a dictating mobster determined to set world morals and she was determined that he wouldn't throw women back to the Dark Ages.

She had then set out to instruct him on the art of sexuality, sensuality and sex in general, coolly pointing out that only a man confined to his hand for pleasure could ever believe that women didn't need or want romance, foreplay, and the freedom to climax as desired.

Amareth couldn't remember anything or anyone who had ever set her brother off with such levels of frustrated rage.

"The minute I get the time, Amareth, I'll show her exactly what I know how to do with my hands," he had snarled. "Right against the cheeks of her well-rounded arse."

She jumped from the chair, quickly keying in the passcode to lock the computer back up before hitting the direct line to Tael's secure communications.

"What?" he answered immediately.

"Get a glider and team ready. I know where he's at."

There was only a second's silence. "We'll be waiting on the pad."

Amareth ran from the room, heading to the roof of the house where the specially designed MacDougal glider awaited them. The latest in weapon, GPS and secure technology graced Mac's personal aircraft. If only he had taken it to the labs instead of the sportier design he had been so eager to try out.

"Where is he?" Tael was waiting in the craft with six of his most trusted men, including Jaime.

Amareth quickly punched the coordinates in on the guidance system before glancing at him with a triumphant expression. "He's gone to show a certain author how The MacDougal deals with impertinent females who make him horny. It's a sexual droid. Programmed to only *fully* function in one manner. Without defrag he had no hope of knowing what was going on, or of processing the information in the mechanical brain. All that is fully processing is his sexuality. Elyiana Richards is his biggest wet dream. He's there taking care of it."

He looked at her incredulously as he took off.

"He's off fucking?" he snapped. "Instead of guarding his arse, he's..."

"Most likely fucking hers," she said dryly. "All the signs were there, but knowing Mac as he was, he would have never gone there. But this is a different side of Mac. Only his sexual side is processing correctly because that's what the droid was created to process best. The rest is scrambled, not easily accessible."

Tael grimaced, punched in several commands and took manual control of the glider. Instantly, booster speed came online and every aerial speed limit on the globe was being broken.

"He was furious at the Richards woman," he snapped. "He was more likely to snap her neck than to fuck her arse."

Amareth snorted at that. "You know Mac as well as I do, Tael, and you remember how damned wild he was before our parents died. You can't repress that sexuality forever without it coming out when least expected. Mac's defenses are down right now, information scrambled in his brain. The sexual droid's preprogramming will be forefront without a defrag. And that programming is sex, period. He's not killing her unless he's fucking her to death."

She glanced at him in time to catch his quick look at her, the flare of arousal in his eyes that was quickly hidden. He never mentioned that hunger, never touched her, but it was always there between them.

"He'll kill us both for this," he finally muttered. "When he's back in his right mind, he'll rip us apart."

Very few things mattered to Mac as much as control, especially control over himself.

Amareth sighed in resignation. "Yes. He will. If you can drag him off his little author long enough."

Chapter Thirteen

The pictures on the computer screen were all beginning to look the same, not to mention the words were beginning to blur. Elyiana closed her eyes and rolled her neck before she stood and stretched her limbs. "I'm sorry Mac, I gotta take a break." She yawned as she moved away from the desk.

Nodding he sat in her chair without taking his eyes off the screen. "Go rest, Legs. I'll search for a while."

"Want another cup of coffee?" she asked over her shoulder

"No, thank ye, love." Brow furrowed, lips pressed together Mac concentrated intently on page after page of missing persons. Quickly he scanned the screen and moved on. Incredibly quickly.

"Okay then, I'm going to go outside and check my garden. I'll be back in a bit." She said watching him warily.

He nodded without looking up, his fingers busily typing, his eyes focused. It all felt right, like it fit. Turning away, she realized it was going to be tough watching him walk away. "Mac."

"Aye," he answered. She waited 'til he raised his head and looked at her.

"All a woman ever wants is to surrender everything she is to the man she chooses to love. It takes an incredibly strong and responsible man to realize what a treasure that is. There aren't many who do." Without waiting for him to respond, she walked out the door.

Love didn't equal weakness, but she was beginning to believe that Mac thought it did. Couldn't he see that it wasn't his strength that made her feel safe with him? And though it was phenomenal, more than the sex she wanted what she saw in his eyes when he let down his guard. The way he was when he held her on the couch. His defenses were down then, he was letting himself feel. What she saw when she looked into his eyes was far more attractive, far more sensuous than the godlike body with the gorgeous face and the never-ending erection. She wanted to know more of the intelligence, the strength and courage she saw there. And there was pain. Sharp and profound that seethed deep inside him. She wanted to touch that too, know it, ease it even if she couldn't heal it.

A slight, fragrant breeze ruffled her hair and she lifted her face to it. She loved the outdoors. The earth, raw and wild, seemed linked with her on some primal level and being a part of her and all that belongs to her gave Elyiana peace. Looking over her thriving plants, she breathed an appreciative sigh. They really were looking lovely, nice and lush. It wouldn't be long 'til they'd be producing. She bent down and pulled the few stray weeds.

Without warning air left her lungs in a whoosh as she was pinned to the ground by a force much like a catapulted brick wall, if there was such a thing. "Get off me." She wheezed when finally she was able to suck in a breath. A split second later a small fireball exploded beside her, directly behind the place where she had stood. She would have been killed. As in dead.

Panic flared to life in her and she struggled beneath the crushing weight, fighting for her freedom only to have Mac's growl in her ear. "Goddammit, Elyiana, be still."

Her eyes widened as she looked up into his face. His expression was savage, murderous. Someone was going to die. He gave her little time to think about that and what she should do next. At lightning speed he was up dragging her to a small thicket and shoved her deep into the brush. Painfully he gripped her shoulders as he shook her to get her attention. "You'll stay here!"

She shook her head. No way was she staying here while he went out there and got himself killed. "No! I'm going with you."

Through gritted teeth he commanded her. "You were nearly killed. You stubborn wench." He shook her again for good measure and she saw it, the desperation. "Stay. Here. I'll no be disobeyed. Do you understand me, Elyiana?" Mesmerized by the swirling emotion she saw in those deep green eyes, she merely nodded.

He kissed her hard and quick then he was gone. Aching from the tackle and the fear, she crouched there trying to see over the bushes without being seen. She couldn't lose him, not like this. Who would want her dead? The MacDougal? He was her only adversary and on more than one occasion she had received furious communications from him. But to kill her, she just couldn't believe he would do something so crass. It would be beneath him to just have her killed. No, he'd maybe shut down his own company to stop her. Cut off his own nose to spite his face so to speak. But The MacDougal wouldn't kill someone unless they absolutely needed killing.

Maybe it had something to do with Mac's past. Where he came from, or escaped from. God, who the hell is he?

Whoever he was, he was hers now and she couldn't stand by and let him get hurt.

* * * * *

Mac moved silently through the thick, twisting vegetation that bordered Elyiana's home, intent on moving behind the assailant and catching him unaware. He could feel a deadly calm settling over his mind, through his body. There was no surging adrenaline, no hard thump of his heart; only his mind seemed to be working quicker. He had pinpointed the area in a second, had even glimpsed the movement of vegetation as the assassin moved to get a better shot.

His senses shifted, his eyesight becoming strangely stronger, his mind working so fast that within seconds he had located the dark form. There was no hesitation in Mac's movements; no delay in his responses. It was odd. He had always worked efficiently in high-pressure situations, even dangerous ones, but this was different. There was something coolly detached between his mind and his body, as though logic and cold hard determination had made his physical self stronger, faster, able to process information more quickly.

He would have questioned it further, if he had the chance. He was only a short distance from his prey now, his eyes narrowed as he moved silently through the underbrush, careful to stay low.

He moved slowly, aware that even the smallest sound, one wrong move could mean his life and Elyiana's. He knew that risking his own was nothing unusual, but he wouldn't risk her. Not for any reason.

Mac weaved his way through the brush, a tight smile crossing his lips as he watched the assailant stiffen, some instinct warning him that he was not alone. That he had become the prey rather than the predator.

As he moved to turn, Mac was on him. In a spurt of speed he rushed the assassin, knocking the lazer rifle from his hands before gripping his head between his forearm, the opposite hand holding him in place as he exerted pressure against the neck while lifting him partially from his feet.

"I don't think so," he bit out tightly, staring into the dark eyes within the confines of the mask that hid his features. "You're caught, bastard."

The man growled, stiffening at the knowledge that there was no escape.

"Who sent you?"

"Fuck you, MacDougal," he snarled. "If I don't kill you someone else will follow me. You're dead."

Shock resounded through him. MacDougal. The MacDougal. He was The MacDougal. The information locked into place like a piece of jigsaw puzzle that suddenly fit.

A chill of foreboding snaked through his mind.

"Who sent you?" he repeated.

"Get fucked."

The flash of steel was the only warning Mac had. The knife cleared the assassin's sleeve heading for Mac's throat. In that instant, Mac let his fury free. With a simple tightening of his arms and a quick jerk, the bastard's neck snapped and he hung silent in Mac's arms.

That was all it took to kill a man.

"Oh my God..." Elyiana's voice had him turning quickly, dropping the body carelessly as his eyes quickly scanned around her to be certain she was okay.

She stood before him, her violet gaze shocked, distressed, watching incredulously.

Her face was so pale her eyes looked like bruised violets in the parchment color. She stared at him in equal parts horror and shock.

"I told you to stay put," he snapped. "Do ye never follow orders, woman?"

He wouldn't have wished for her to see this. Would have avoided it at all costs. Mac knew there was a core of mercilessness inside him, something broken, something that had been destroyed within him. He had no regrets for killing the bastard. The assassin would have killed Elyiana with pleasure, perhaps would have tortured her first. That's what they did. They tortured their women in front of the men sworn to protect them. They broke limbs, left slashing wounds, they raped with no regard to the horror left in the minds of those forced to witness it.

"Mac..." She shook her head slowly, her gaze trained on his upper arm, so filled with anguish that it struck his soul with pain.

His gaze sliced to his arm as he tilted his shoulder forward. He blinked, certain he couldn't see what he thought he was seeing, certain that somehow this was some terrible nightmare, some twist to reality that could be easily fixed. But he knew better. In that second, in one blinding horrible moment of clarity, it all came back to him.

"I'll fuckin' kill her."

Chapter Fourteen

Struggling to free herself from Mac's grip, Elyiana ran to keep up as he pulled her along behind him.

"Wait, Mac," she shouted. The shock was fading, giving way to the need for comprehension.

"We have to go. Now." The statement was delivered in a cold, level voice. It was stern and distant, leaving no room for argument or negotiation.

Inside the house he shut the door and locked it. His mind was clearly focused on the task at hand, his expression set in stone, his jaw clenched. Elyiana fought to make sense of the cybernetics she'd seen beneath Mac's skin. Incredible advances had been made in the field of cybertronics and android technology. There had to be a reasonable explanation for it.

"Have you had an accident? Maybe you've had an arm replaced." Reaching out, her voice hoarse with fear, she stepped toward him.

Warmth met her light touch. She let her hand slide upward to the wound in his shoulder. Even now he was warm but not hot. After wrestling with the assassin outside in the smoldering heat he should be sweaty or at least hot. But he wasn't. Never had he broken a sweat, not once.

"Too high on the shoulder to be just an arm, Elyiana. Dress yourself in something more appropriate. We must leave. Now."

"No, Mac. Let's wait for Scott. He can help us," she said cautiously. With an almost imperceptible grimace, he moved away from her. "There must be some reasonable explanation for it." She voiced what her mind was screaming at her.

Bewildered at his complete withdrawal from her she stepped purposefully closer. He'd suddenly gone remote, cold. Her throat constricted with fear, her heart clenched in her chest. Looking up, her gaze collided with his and she forgot to breathe. There, in his eyes she saw fury, fear. In his eyes, she could see the questions they both wanted to ask but were afraid to face. A myriad of emotions swirled within them like a misty emerald lake. And she saw Mac.

Pressing her hand to his chest feeling the slow and steady rhythm of his heart as it pumped blood through his body. No, she breathed deeply, it should be faster, at least a bit. The anger glowing in his eyes now should cause blood to race through his veins. Glancing at the wound she frowned, but there was no blood. His heart should be pounding against his breastbone. Thinking back to the many bouts of hot sex, the intense energy he'd exerted, she couldn't remember one time when she felt his heart pound.

Grabbing her by the shoulders he pulled her against him. "You'll do as I say now, Elyiana. I'll no wait around for the pup and risk both of our necks. D'ye understand me?" he said smoothly, his face devoid of expression except for his eyes.

"Mac." Without looking away she tried to reason with him. "We can continue to scan the missing persons files."

He stepped closer to her, his jaw tightening. "It doesna matter now."

Blinking, Elyiana backed up a step. "Listen to me." She sighed with frustration. "We can search the news reports." The labs had nearly perfected the new sex droids but she thought they hadn't been able to get them up and running…so to speak. Reportedly they were still doing research.

Mac looked down at her, his brow slowly lifting. "Are ye afraid, Legs?" he asked huskily.

Elyiana watched his eyes, the emotion that warred in them. Yes she was afraid. Afraid of what he was, what he wasn't. But she wasn't a coward.

"No. I'm not afraid of you," she snapped. "But we need to find out who you are. To find out if you…if you're…"

Cocking his head to the side he watched her with a cold smile. "If I'm what, Legs? If I'm human? If I'm real?"

Advancing on her, Mac's eyes never left hers. Elyiana couldn't help but retreat instinctually even though she knew he wouldn't hurt her. The fierceness there in his eyes was enough to make her tremble anyway. She shook her head in denial of what he was saying. In her heart she knew he was real, so very real, but the inconsistencies had to be worked out. They had to find answers. All along she knew something wasn't quite right. Why didn't she use her head for once instead of moving forward with what was in her heart, her soul and spirit?

Frantically she tried to think, reason things out but as her back met the cool solidity of the wall, Mac's mouth covered hers, savagely demanding, taking. His body pressed her firmly against the wall. Framing her face, his hands held her still as his tongue sought hers, staking claim. Finally he lifted his head and she tried to catch her breath, reclaim her sanity as desire surged through her. Immediately, her body responded, swelling, tightening. Moisture gathered and flooded her pussy.

Mac looked down at her narrowing his eyes. "Does that no feel real to ye, Legs?" Without warning, his hands slid down over her chest and cupped her breasts as he squeezed her taut nipples. "Does this?" he asked with a growl as he gripped the neckline of the delicate sundress and tore it from her body leaving her naked save for her panties.

With the groan of a tortured man he lifted her, wrapping her legs around his hips. Bracing his legs apart, his lips crushed hers, urging them open. Engulfed in the flash fire of his passion, Elyiana's hands fisted in his hair, devouring him, taking as much as he'd give. Her heart thudded so hard she was sure it would shatter from the sheer force. Before she had time to think, Mac ripped her panties free of her body and pushed the wide head of his cock inside her convulsing pussy.

Lowering his head, Mac bit her neck, drawing on her ultra-sensitive skin as he pushed inside, invading her, stretching her open. Every time, every single time felt like the first. Elyiana gasped, pleasure stealing her breath, her thoughts fractured as the sensation of him moving inside her overwhelmed everything else. She wanted all of him, every thick inch. Loved the way he invaded her, stretched her open. Yes, he was real, so real. She never doubted it. No robot, no android had a spirit, but she'd felt Mac's spirit from the very beginning. Tightening her legs around him she tilted her hips, taking him deeper as she hissed through the sting of her over-stimulated flesh, stretching to accommodate the girth of his shaft. Just a small bite of pain but it was glorious; she wanted more.

"*Mo' Dia*," he groaned. "Ellie, you're so fuckin' tight."

Why was he always so careful? Damn him, he was driving her insane. "More, Mac, give me more, give me all," she demanded as she arched against him, rubbing her tight nipples against his chest. All, and nothing less but she feared that whatever this was, whatever was wrong might have caused him to retreat from her forever. Desperately she clung to him with her body, her mind, her soul.

He thrust into her then and she cried out, her nails biting into his scalp as she began to ride him. He smacked her ass as he braced his legs further apart and picked up the pace. "Mmm, yes Mac, yes," she whimpered.

Savagely he pounded into her, his fingers digging into the flesh of her hips, his mouth ravaging hers between whispering things in Gaelic that could have meant anything but was so damn sexy she thought she'd come from the words themselves. The muscled walls of her vagina contracted around him as he hammered into her. Sensations began overlapping, coiling tighter and tighter inside her. All too soon they splintered, sending shards of pleasure shooting from the core of her, outward. Shuddering through the devastating orgasm she screamed his name, clutching at him as the ecstasy wrapped around her again.

It was just as her second climax crested and Mac's head fell back as she took him over the brink with her that Scott swung the door open. Taking in the scene, his good-humored greeting died on his tongue.

Chapter Fifteen

It wasn't natural. Mac was well aware of the speed he used in lifting Elyiana from his still erect cock, setting her aside and jumping for the intrusive male. Protecting her was uppermost in his mind, keeping her safe from harm first, keeping her alive and breathing, rather than the shell of a human as he knew he was.

The rage of that realization wasn't pumping through his veins but it was burning through his mind, his mechanical heart, his soul. He wanted to howl with the fury of it, wanted to rip at the long hair sprouting from his head until he broke into the computerized brain and jerked the memories from them. How the hell had this happened? Why had Amareth allowed it?

And she had allowed it.

Within a second the bastard was gasping, struggling, lifted inches from his feet and pinned to the wall as he stared back at Mac in horror. Blue eyes were bulging helplessly, darkly tanned face paling as the muscular young man fought the hold. He should have been strong enough to break free. He was younger, as fit as Mac, and too damned heavy to be holding like this for any length of time. But Mac felt no strain on his muscles, no burning, no stress. Holding the full-grown man to the wall as he kicked and bucked against the hold required no effort at all.

"Ellie," the stranger gasped helplessly, his eyes bugging and flying frantically to Elyiana for help.

"Mac, stop!" Her furious scream was a shock to his senses. Her voice should be filled with the afterglow of pleasure, not fear, not anger.

"It's Scott, Mac. Please. Damn you, let him go!" A resounding kick, one that should have caused at least a twinge of pain, was delivered to his shin.

"Let him go." She stared up at him, enraged now, her violet eyes blazing back at him in shock and censure.

Slowly, Mac looked back at the male he held pinned to the wall. His face was beginning to darken, a sure sign that he needed air desperately. Slowly, Mac released the blond, Scott, the same man who had dared fondle Elyiana days before. That alone was reason enough to kill the bastard.

He was coughing, heaving for breath as Mac slowly stepped back.

"You should be a wee bit more careful about sneakin' up on a man," he snapped, grabbing Elyiana's arm when she would have rushed for her friend.

"Let me go, Neanderthal," she snapped belligerently as she jerked at her arm.

Mac looked down at the slender limb he held. His hold wasn't so tight that she should've have been able to jerk free easily. But there she was, trapped by his fingers, unable to jerk free.

Deliberately he released her.

"Did you bring the clothes?" he asked the other man, little caring that he was still fighting for breath.

His mind was consumed with the sudden realizations slamming into it, rather than the angry looks he was receiving from Elyiana and her friend.

There were still gaps of information, things that made no sense, but other things made more than enough sense.

"Who is this bastard, Ellie?" Scott wheezed as Elyiana cast him a dark, accusing look.

"We're not certain yet," she soothed her friend, though she watched Mac.

Naked. Damn her, she was still naked, sheened with sweat from the exertion of climaxing in his arms and she hadn't even noticed. She was as comfortable with her nudity as she was in being dressed. Or just too damned pissed off to care. He wondered which it was.

Her dark eyes made him want to hit something. They were filled with fear and betrayal, and knowledge. He could see the knowledge, just as he felt his.

"You're certain," he said softly then, denying her words to the other man. "Get dressed. I'll no have you parading naked around that bastard."

"It won't be the first time," she snapped furiously, her face blazing with color.

Rage surged through him unlike anything he could ever remember feeling.

"D'ye no want him to live, Legs?" he snarled, barely holding onto his control now as he spied the bags the man had dropped just inside the door.

Several articles of clothing spilled from them. Soft khaki pants and a loose shirt. Shoes.

He stepped over and jerked the bag from the floor before he gripped her arm once again, staring into her shocked face as he fought the impulses going crazy inside him. Possessiveness, jealousy, a fear of losing her.

"We have to go." He tried to soften his voice from an order to a demand. "That assassin wouldna be alone, Elyiana, you know that. You aren't safe here."

"But am I any safer with you?"

He hated the doubt he could hear in her voice.

"I'll never harm ye," he swore, hating the fact that he had already. "But I won't leave ye alone here, either. And I won't be responsible for my own rage if you dinna get your pretty arse dressed now!" He snapped off the order, realizing he was making an ass of himself and his own vows to never let a woman touch his heart in such a way.

"Primitive, aren't you, mate?" Scott gasped as Elyiana moved slowly toward the bedroom, but Mac noticed the other man kept his eyes firmly off her delicious ass.

"Possessive." He jerked the clothes from the bag and began dressing quickly. "You had a four-seater the other day. Are ye piloting the same glider?"

"You aren't taking my baby," Scott bit out, his blue eyes snapping with his own fury now. "You got the girl; leave the damned glider alone."

"The girl is mine and the damned glider is the only thing standing between her and another assassin," he snarled as he jerked the pants on over his lean hips.

"Assassin?" Scott shook his head incredulously, rubbing absently at his abraded throat. "Don't tell me The MacDougal finally snapped and tried to kill her?"

There was an edge of mocking humor in the man's voice that Mac found more than offensive.

"The MacDougal does not hire assassins to take out romance writers," he informed the other man sarcastically. "He saves them for real enemies, like smart-arsed outbackers without the sense to do as they're told."

Scott shook his head with a short, disbelieving laugh. "Damn me, you sound just like the bastard."

"And so I should." Mac narrowed his eyes as he jerked the dark tan shirt over his head and watched the other man carefully. "I am The MacDougal."

A movement from the corner of his eye had him turning slowly. Elyiana stood in her bedroom doorway, staring back at him, her eyes wide, but not in shock. No, it wasn't shock brightening her beautiful violet eyes, it was pain and tears.

She had dressed in soft leggings and a short, snug top that cupped her breasts lovingly. On her feet, were soft ankle boots, similar to his own, laced snugly on her feet and well worn from use.

"Ellie, do you hear his mad claims?" Scott was laughing incredulously. "The MacDougal is a good deal older and a hell of a lot less primitive. I hope you haven't let him convince you of this hogwash."

Mac ignored the pesky little male. Scott was likely a good enough man on a better day, but today, he was doing no more than making a bad situation worse.

"We have to leave, Legs," he whispered. "We have to get out of here until I can figure out what the hell is going on."

He knew his life and hers were in more danger than he could ever convince her of. The very fact that he was standing in the body of the new technological miracle that his scientists put together, proved his own suspicions the week before. Because of this he had been attacked and nearly killed. There was a traitor in his company, and Mac knew it. That was the reason he had been rushing for the labs when he was attacked, to view the model and learn if it was as advanced as Amareth had assured him it was in her reports. Reports that someone else had somehow accessed.

"Elyiana." He ignored Scott, holding his hand out to her. He wouldn't beg, but he wouldn't leave without her. Not now, not ever. "Surely, Legs, you wouldna leave me on this final path alone? Not now." Not trapped inside a body not his own.

He watched as she swallowed tightly, her gaze flickering to Scott before coming back to him.

"I'm going to kill you when all this is over with," she whispered wrathfully. "Slowly, painfully, I'm going to make you pay."

He sighed roughly. "*Mo cridhe,* if they can't fix what they've wrought here then I'll gladly supply you the weapons. Now let's get the hell out of here."

He snagged the gun he had laid earlier on the kitchen table, turning for the door.

"Trust you to find a girl, a fight and an assassin." He froze at the low, drawling amusement in the dark female voice. "If you weren't anyone but my brother, I might suspect you were having a good time here."

Mac turned slowly. He saw the strain in the young woman's face, the concern in Tael's eyes as he stood behind her protectively.

Scott was backing away from the door, obviously placing himself with Mac, in front of Elyiana who was slowly moving forward.

"You know, Am," he drawled then. "Tanning your hide is going to be a pleasure. I believe you're long overdue. Now can you fucking fix it?"

Her gaze flickered with a little less confidence than he was hoping for.

"We think we can."

He frowned as he absently pushed Scott back and pulled Elyiana forward, his arm going around her waist.

"You better pray you can, lass," he said softly, warningly. "Otherwise, there's a promise I'm goin' to be breaking and an arse I'm going to be paddlin'. Remember that one well."

He stared at her, watching her as her eyes widened, the threat sinking home. The spanking wouldn't bother her. The promise would terrify her.

Chapter Sixteen

The MacDougal turned his hard gaze back to Elyiana as she scrambled for understanding through the rage and the pain. No, that wasn't right. Maybe his body was close to the same but not the face, and The MacDougal's eyes were lighter. But he was there now, in those dark angry eyes filled with rabid determination. Why had she never seen it? "Let's go. Now, Ellie."

Elyiana shook her head. "Fix what?" A sense of foreboding swirled through her brain making her feel dizzy, displaced. Her hands clenched at her sides, she looked from Mac, to Amareth, back to him. Sure her heart was about to rip in two from the force of it all, she stepped around Scott and ignored whatever it was he was saying to her. "Someone better explain," she demanded as she jerked away from Mac's attempt to touch her. All she wanted, needed, were answers, anything close to reasonable, to make sense of what was happening.

Amareth MacDougal, the infamous ball-busting bitch shifted from one foot to another, intently studying her. A heady mixture of fury, fear and bone-deep hurt radiated from the siblings in dark waves. Elyiana had always known there was much more to Amareth than what she presented to the world. Standing by her now she was torn between wanting to wrap her arms around her and punch her in the gut.

This couldn't be an elaborate plan to shut her up, to shut her down. It just didn't make sense. True, The

MacDougal was livid that she'd ignored him, even gone so far as to laugh in his face. Surely he wouldn't go this far. Or was this his demented attempt at proving her to be the fool he thought she was? To show her how destructive her "romantic notions" could be. But there was a dead man in her yard. She'd watched Mac kill him with his bare hands.

Then the wound on his shoulder. Oh God. Dismissing the rationalizations plaguing her brain, Elyiana turned to Amareth. Standing eye to eye with her, Elyiana could swear she saw respect and admiration in their emerald depths. Her voice, however, demanded timely obedience. "No time, Ms. Richards. We must leave now."

Lifting a brow, she crossed her arms and took a step back. "I'm not going anywhere. Especially without knowing exactly what the hell is going on."

"Och aye, you'll go." Mac narrowed his eyes.

Still rubbing at his bruised throat, Scott bravely put an arm around her shoulders. It was an incredibly self-sacrificing move on his part and Elyiana knew it. So did Scott. Yet he pulled her protectively closer to his stiff body. "Bloody hell," Scott grumbled with exasperation, spearing his fingers through his mussed blond hair. "You damned dolt, you think because you had a naughty with 'er you own her?"

An audible rumble came from low in Mac's chest as he bared his teeth and took a step toward Scott. Releasing Elyiana, Scott widened his stance, lifted his chin and prepared himself for the fight he was certain would come. Elyiana grabbed his shirt and tried to pull him back. When she couldn't, she put herself between them.

"Get out o' the way, Elyiana," Mac commanded as he grasped her shoulders. He was always commanding something or other.

"Yeah, Ellie, move out of the way. I'm not afraid of the arsehole. He's just a show pony," Scott snarled.

"Damn it, Scott!" she cried out, struggling to hold him back. "Stop it!"

Scott was a large man, and muscular to boot. But Elyiana was quite sure The MacDougal could pummel him to dust. That wasn't something she was willing to watch happen. "Why can't you just leave us? The assassin was after Mac, not me. Just go."

"That's right. I'm here. She'll be apples with me. Just like she was before you came around. It'd be best if you just take your thugs and rack off, MacDougal." Scott's voice was low and hoarse with anger.

"Stop, Mac," Amareth said without looking away from Elyiana. Mac's hands fisted at his side as he glared at them. But he stopped, barely. Elyiana could swear she could see his big body vibrating with fury. "Ms. Richards, eventually everything will be explained. At this point in time you aren't safe here. They know The MacDougal was here. They'll do whatever it takes to find out where he went. We will not leave you here to endure the very creative and excruciating torture they will have for you and your…friend."

"You're telling me I have no choice? Is that it?" Elyiana demanded.

"No. You have a choice," Amareth said darkly as she turned and walked briskly out the door.

"She's right. I'll give you a choice, love." Mac's voice was deceptively calm. "Either you'll come under your own power or I'll carry ye to the transport. Either way, you're comin' wi me."

"I don't trust you," she said through clenched teeth.

"I know." There it was once again, in those strange emerald eyes. Regret, resignation, fear. Bloody hell.

"This is your fault. You've brought this on her, you Goddamned fool!" Scott shouted at Mac. Elyiana stomped Scott's foot when she couldn't hold him back. He never even flinched.

"Tell me, Mac, what's happened?" she whispered.

"You'll know the all of it soon enough, Ellie." Mac's voice hardened as he met the gaze of the man who stood behind her now. Through narrowing eyes he stared at him, the muscle in his jaw working.

"We have to leave now, Mac," the tall, dark-haired man who'd stood beside Amareth said impatiently.

Mac took her upper arm in his hand and pulled her roughly away from Scott.

"NO." This time she couldn't free herself from his grasp. Two men flanked Scott and led him forcibly out the door. "Tell me now. I'm not going 'til someone gives me some answers."

Mac swung her around and she collided into his chest. His mouth took hers in a kiss that demanded her response. She pushed at his chest as the tears burned her eyes. He cupped her cheek, his thumb caressing the corner of her mouth urging her lips apart. She tasted his desperation as his tongue stroked hers. More than anything she wanted to submit to him, wrap her arms around him and give back. But she couldn't, not now, possibly not ever again. He was The MacDougal. He took what he wanted. The hurt was too big; it was overwhelming her.

Pushing him away, she gasped for breath. She was so angry. Angry that he betrayed her, that he lied. Angry that she had been so gullible, so weak. "I'll never forgive you for this." Her voice was hoarse with emotion as silent tears streamed down her face.

His eyes narrowed with what she thought was pain. But that couldn't be, The MacDougal had no heart. "It doesna change anything," he said huskily. She swallowed hard, intently watching him. "Let's go, Legs." Looking away he all but dragged her from her home.

She lifted her chin defiantly as she tried to keep up with him. "Once again *The MacDougal* gets his way," she said quietly. "Underneath it all you're just a bully."

The glider was state of the art. Built for comfort as well as speed. Mac wouldn't let her sit next to Scott. But he had caught her eye long enough to mouth "sorry" to her. Elyiana just shook her head. Scott had done his best to protect her, had even risked life and limb to do so. But she would have done the same for him. He'd been there for her when she had no one else. They had explored their feelings for each other. Romantically speaking they didn't gel quite right, but she loved him, not as a lover but as something stronger than a mere physical relationship. He was her friend. She would not allow The MacDougal or anyone else to hurt Scott, not without a fight.

Mac sat with Amareth now, speaking in voices too quiet to understand. And by the looks on their faces, that was no easy task. Mac had tied his hair back, the shadows played on his face in the dim light and she could see the resemblance. Very slight but it was there. It was hard to understand how she could have missed it. One sees what one wants to see, she supposed. Perhaps it had always been there between her and The MacDougal. For months there had been passion between them, of one sort or the other.

She had found herself looking forward to the angry emails and the heated debates on the communicator screen. She'd even gone so far as to put him in her stories. Fantasized about him, hot steamy fantasies that didn't hold a candle to the real thing. Even more than that, though, she'd connected to Mac on a level she never even knew existed, as much as she hated to admit it. And perhaps that was why it all hurt so badly.

Exceptional circumstances have a way of changing things. In his eyes she'd seen the man with whom she thought she was falling in love. Closing her eyes, she laid her head back against her seat and fought the knot of pain that threatened to choke her. This couldn't be happening to her. She'd go to sleep and when she woke up she'd be in her own bed with one hell of a story to write. And maybe, just maybe, the pain would be gone.

The dream was relentless and heart-wrenching. Mac touching her, loving her. His mouth moved over her, giving her pleasure so intense. His hands, rougher, they were rougher than before. More rugged than before, his face stronger. Her fingertips traced the scar on his cheek as he drew on her nipple. She arched against him and looked down into his sea green eyes. "*Ghrá mo cridhe*," he murmured against her trembling flesh.

The pain came back like a flood and she moaned as a strong hand stroked her cheek, so tenderly coaxing her awake. Slowly she opened her eyes to find Mac leaning over her, his mouth so close to hers, whispering. What had he said? "What?" she rasped harshly. Frowning, she took a deep breath as she pushed him away. Purposefully breaking the erotic spell that had begun to whirl about her, within her. It was best not to surrender to that again.

"We're about to land," he said stiffly, settling back into his seat.

Without answering she shifted in her seat, scowling at the tendrils of sensation that spiraled upward as the slick folds of her pussy rasped against her damp panties. Clenching her teeth she also resisted the urge to rub at her erect nipples. She wanted to scream with frustration. Hadn't she been happy before he'd climbed through her bedroom window? Damn him for making her want more than she could have. Damn that stupid dream. Damn, damn, damn.

The glider flew gracefully into the hanger and landed smoothly. Mac stood and reached for Elyiana as she unbuckled her seatbelt. "Don't. Touch me," she snarled at him. The muscle in his jaw clenched, his eyes flashed, there was no time to think or react as he reached down taking her by her shoulders and lifted her from her seat.

In a second, she found herself dangling inches above the glider floor, nose to nose with the bane of her existence. "No matter how you hate me, lass; no matter if you ne'r forgive me. It doesna matter. You're mine and you'll no tell me not to touch you."

His mouth closed over hers in a kiss of possession, his tongue staking his claim on her. Elyiana struggled to free herself, whimpering as he finally let her go and sat her away from him. The look on his face was savage, full of lust and pain. "Best you no forget that, Legs. Ever!"

Turning away, he stalked from the glider. Amareth met her gaze and if she didn't know better she saw a spark of sympathy there. The corner of Amareth's mouth twitched just a bit before she followed her brother.

Chapter Seventeen

He had lived through one of the most tumultuous periods of the reconstruction of worldwide democracy. He had survived the attempt on his life when his parents were killed and managed to not just rescue his brother and sister, but to raise them alongside him and protect everything the Clan MacDougal had claimed as their own.

He had fought tooth and nail, ruthlessly squelching inborn morals and a sense of right and wrong to assure that his family survived and that it survived intact. Never again he had sworn, would he allow those bloody rebels to steal more from him than they already had. And in the end, it had come to this.

He was slowly remembering everything. His childhood, the massacre of the MacDougal and McLeod families, his steady, determined rise to the position of power he had attained. And now it was all threatened. His very sense of himself had been stolen because of a rebel's bullets.

"I can't believe ye did this, Am." He stood in the lab now, staring down at his still, silent body, fear unlike anything he had ever known welling inside him.

"I can't believe you're taking it so hard," she snapped back, though he heard the hurt in her voice. "If you had stayed put like you were supposed to, the cybernetic brain would have defragged and you would have been just fine until we could have effected another transfer."

"Don't talk to me as though I were a child, girl," he snarled, turning back on her, his eyes narrowing as she squared her shoulders and braced herself for the fight she thought was coming.

Had he done this to her? He had never laid a hand on her. Hell, he hadn't even spanked her when she was a wee thing. But he had raised her hard, he knew that. Taught her to fend for herself, to fight for herself, to be strong. Or had he stripped her of something he had never meant to?

"Fuck!" He cursed savagely as he turned away from her, clenching his fists on the glass partition between him and his body. "Goddamn, Amareth. I'm a fucking robot and ye stand there like I shouldn't know any fury for it."

Fury he knew well. It was raging in his mind, sparking an inner rage he feared he couldn't contain.

"It was the only way," she informed him coolly, and he realized in that moment how much he hated to hear that in her voice.

As a child, Am had laughed harder than the rest of them, played with more joy and knew a sense of dreams that had amazed him as a young man. Where had that warmth, that passion in her voice gone? When had it disappeared?

Damn it all to hell. He rubbed at his neck, feeling the flesh there, the warmth of the friction and had to fight the need to pretend it was real. He wanted nothing more than to turn away from the silent form of his body in that fucking stasis unit and return to Elyiana, bury himself in her warmth, feel her hot and wet around his cock as he filled her, kept her screaming with pleasure and with need.

"Transference won't be easy," he said bleakly, allowing the information he managed to locate on the process to sift through his mind. "I don't know how you made it work the first time."

"I didn't make it work," she told him tightly. "You did. Only information was supposed to transfer. We've run it over a hundred times. This is the first time transference has occurred this way. You knew you were dying, Mac. You made the choice yourself."

He turned to her again; he couldn't help himself. She stood there across the room, alone. She was frowning at him, her green eyes snapping with ire, the light freckles across her cheeks and nose reminding him of the child she had once been. A child who had demanded hugs and kisses, who had spun dreams and fantasies. There was no evidence of that child now.

What the hell had he done to her? What the hell had he done to himself?

"How long before we can attempt transference again?" he asked her, breathing in deeply in an effort to contain within his mind the conflicting impulses attacking him.

"Your body has nearly finished healing." She shrugged, crossing her arms over her breasts as she stumbled over the word, body. "We need to put you through defrag, to be certain everything is in order."

He shook his head roughly.

"Defrag will cement the information into the droid's brain. It could possibly hold the rest of me here as well. I don't want to attempt it."

"For God's sake Mac, can't you trust me to fucking do anything right?" She snapped back at him, furious then.

"This wasn't your baby, it was mine. I've been on it since its inception. I know this model backward and forward and you're still treating me like a child."

He watched her silently, seeing the flush that mantled her cheeks as her anger began to spike.

"True," he smiled tightly. "And kept me in the dark for the most part. When did ye intend to tell me, sister dear, that you made a damned near replica of me in this sex droid of yours?"

Her eyes narrowed. "I actually intended to wait until we unveiled the model to your board," she informed him coldly. "You're so damned concerned with the bottom line that you would have never noticed what it looked like, only how it performed."

He wanted to roll his eyes but refrained. "And why me?" he snapped. "Why not Tael?"

She arched a brow mockingly, her eyes glittering with pleasure.

"You think you're the only model?" she drawled then. "Really Mac, I love you dearly, but I have no desire to fuck you. And I do have all intentions of benefiting from the design."

He was speechless. He stared back at her in shock. He had never expected her to get back at Tael in such a way. Unfortunately, he knew the other man well. If Tael ever learned what Amareth had done, he would rip the droid apart limb by limb before he showed Amareth just exactly why she needed a man rather than a toy.

"Fuck," he breathed out slowly. "Tael will kill you."

She lifted her shoulder negligently. "He has to find out first. And you might be pissed, but I don't think you would actually tell on me."

Her gaze was direct, and beneath the cool exterior he glimpsed the imp she used to be. Damn her, Tael would strangle her with his bare hands but Mac couldn't help but share in her amusement. She was a bold, brazen little lass when she had to be.

"Brat." He allowed the corner of his mouth to twitch into the smile he would have otherwise hidden as he used the pet name for her that he had used when she was a child.

He saw her surprise, watched her firm her own lips to fight back her grin.

"Be that as it may." She cleared her throat firmly as she faced him, her arms uncrossing to allow her thumbs to hook into the snug waistband of her pants. "I've been going over the schematics as well as the computer analysis of the moments you transferred completely into the droid. The energy spike was slight, but it was there. I know what to look for. And all my findings lead me to believe that if you don't allow the defrag then there's no chance in hell we're going to get you back where you belong."

Mac gritted his teeth, allowing a small, rumbling growl to vibrate from his chest. Or rather, the android's chest. Damn, she had done a good job, even if he did know he wasn't real.

"Amareth, if you don't get me out of this fucking body, so help me God, I'm going to tell Tael everything I know," he snapped furiously, knowing he wouldn't, no matter what happened, but the threat was there. He had taught her the value of a good threat himself.

"If this doesn't work, Mac, then I expect nothing less," she said wearily. "But I stand behind my decision. When you transferred into the droid, it somehow allowed us to place you deeper into stasis. Without that option, you would be dead anyway. At least this way, you're alive."

"Is that what ye call it?" he snapped, spearing her with a hard look. "This isn't so lively, Am. It's damned uncomfortable."

She snorted mockingly. "From the look of Ms. Richards, I would say she's enjoyed it immensely. Who knew the droid's programming was so damned good? Your first thought on waking was to fuck. I just never imagined you would go so far for it."

She slanted him a questioning glance, but Mac kept his mouth firmly shut. He knew why he had gone to Elyiana, why she had seemed familiar and yet a stranger. Just as he knew why his first thought was to fuck the little witch into submission. She had bewitched him with those damned books, just as she had the rest of the world.

"When do I go into defrag?" he asked instead.

Amareth shrugged. "Sooner the better. We don't have a lot of time. You've been in the droid's housing for almost a week now. We need to get you out of there."

He glanced back at his own body, but he thought of Elyiana. His Legs. The woman who had bewitched him, stolen his heart, and taught him to dream again. All before he had ever met her.

"Am." He tapped his fingers against the glass shield. "If this doesn't work, you take care of her. You hear me?"

He didn't turn back to her, but he could feel her. The sharpness of her gaze, the questions she must have running through her head.

"It will work," she finally said firmly.

"You heard me. Now promise me." She would never break a promise to him.

"You know I will, Mac. Do you think I don't know you've fallen in love with her?" she asked sadly. "I know you, brother. I know what I saw. I'll make certain she stays safe."

He nodded bleakly. "Let's get on with it, dammit. I'm tired of occupying this fucking pile of electronics and wires you placed me into. I want my own body back if you don't mind too much."

The lab door suddenly slammed furiously. Surprised, Mac turned to see Elyiana, her gaze snapping with her anger, her body stiff with tension.

"Before you do any damned thing, you're going to explain this to me, MacDougal." She pointed an imperious little finger at him, her violet eyes smoldering with rage. "Right here, right now, by God, or I'm going to kill you myself."

Mac wanted to smile. He wanted to go to her, wrap her in his arms, hold her and convince her as well as himself, that everything was going to work, that soon, he would be himself. He wanted to tell her he loved her. And God help him, he wanted to hear her say the same.

"Confine her to her rooms," he ordered Amareth instead. "Then get back here and we'll get started."

He turned his back on both of them and stalked into the connecting labs before he lost all sense of control and himself. The thought of losing Elyiana was more frightening than the thought of never holding her again. But even worse was the thought that he would never return to her as himself, rather than the machine. That, he couldn't bear.

Chapter Eighteen

"Confine me to my…" Elyiana's eyes widened, her mouth opened, as she lost all will to rein in her anger. "Like hell!" Following fast on Mac's heels she glared at Amareth, who wisely lifted her hands and stepped back. "You son of a bitch!" Elyiana snarled. Her hand fisted in his shirt and tugged as hard as she could. The fabric ripped as she forced him to turn and face her.

"This is none of your concern, Elyiana," Mac replied, his eyes cold, devoid of emotion as he stepped away from her. Distancing himself. Well it was way too late for that. Too much had happened in such a short period of time. Had it really only been a few days? It felt like a lifetime.

"The hell it isn't!" she snapped. "You broke into my home, took the help I offered you, put me and my friend in danger."

"Och aye, that is precisely why you'll be kept here. Until it's safe for you to leave." Like a flash fire, his cool aloof façade disintegrated. With his hair hung loose again, his nostrils flared, he had that lion-like look. Hungry, predatory, dangerous. His fingers wrapped around her upper arm leading her back to the room where Amareth stood.

God no, he couldn't leave her this way. Not without answers.

"No!" Fighting against him she planted her feet and wrenched her arm from his grasp. Elyiana felt her throat closing, her eyes stung. Taking a deep breath, she looked up at him. "My God, Mac. You've had your cock buried so deep inside me there were moments I felt as though you'd become part of me." Panting for breath she squared her shoulders. Shaking her head she held his gaze, searching for the man. Her throat ached, her voice was low and gravely. "That makes this my fucking concern."

"Goddammit to bloody hell, Elyiana!" he roared. Spinning away from her, he plowed his fist through a wall. She couldn't help flinching but held her ground and tried vehemently to still the tremors that racked her body. Mac pulled his fist from the wall and looked at it as if it weren't a part of him "Fuck," he grumbled then shook the drywall dust from his knuckles.

"We have a breach." Amareth said softly as she leaned against the doorframe.

"Shut up, Am," Mac warned through clenched teeth.

"She deserves answers, Mac," she appealed to him. Mac glared at her, openly hostile.

For a moment, Elyiana thought he might just cross the room, snag Amareth up and toss her out on her ass. Instead, he speared a hand through his hair and nodded for her to carry on. "Fine."

"As I was saying there was a breach, a mole, traitor if you will," Amareth continued, all the while watching her brother cautiously.

"I'm not an idiot; you don't have to give me a damned thesaurus," Elyiana snipped. The tension was making her want to yank her hair out. "Just…"she paused, squeezing her eyes shut for a second, then looked back to Amareth. "Just tell me."

With a nod, Amareth continued to detail for her the events leading up to their attempt to save Mac. It felt as thought her heart would implode as what she had begun to suspect was made truth. Everything in her struggled against it, wanting to believe it was a lie, it couldn't be true. Pain knotted in her stomach, pain and fear. Still, she fought to assimilate the information, to acknowledge what she was hearing and process it as fact.

Since the assassin's attack she'd tried to understand the wound, the cybernetics. The way he was sexually, his stamina, his ejaculation, his lack of sweat. The way he ate, the peculiar way he could immediately fall asleep and wake up and was never tired. There had to be a reasonable explanation. But what she'd come up with just couldn't be right. No, she wouldn't accept the things her mind was screaming at her. He was real, she'd felt him, she had looked into his eyes and seen the man she could fall in love with.

The strange unexplainable things that had been warning her all along made sense now. What she'd feared to be true from the moment she saw the cybernetics in his shoulder was actually true. The man she had welcomed into her home, into her body was not a man but a…machine. A sex droid.

But she had watched his eyes darken with desire. The things he'd whispered to her while he moved inside her, driving her to madness, no robot would say that. A very convincing sex droid. The need to cry out, to deny what she was hearing clawed at Elyiana's throat. She bit her lip to contain it and focused on what Amareth was telling her.

"We didn't expect it to happen the way it did. But without complete transference we would have been unable to save Mac." Amareth's voice seemed far off as though she spoke through a veil of fog.

"So you're telling me that Mac's spirit transferred into the droid along with the contents of his brain?" She could feel Mac watching her but she couldn't look at him. Not yet.

"We believe so," Amareth answered matter-of-factly. Elyiana studied her as she explained. "We believe…"

"Who is 'we'?" Elyiana asked, her voice too rough, too weak.

Amareth met her gaze, then with a sigh continued. "I believe Mac knew on a subconscious level that he was dying and rebelled against it. By using the force of his unyielding stubborn will, he chose to throw everything he is into surviving. And he did." Elyiana continued to stare at Amareth. Trying so hard to believe the unbelievable. Amareth shifted uncomfortably and uncrossed her arms. "I've conferred with the team on it and they concur."

Finally she turned her head and met his gaze. "Can you fix it?" Elyiana asked softly. She wanted him whole, even though she suddenly knew that once he was whole he wouldn't want her. He'd been locked in the body of a sex droid. No wonder he couldn't get enough of her.

She looked back at Amareth in time to see the irritation flicker in her eyes. "We think…"

Elyiana held up a hand. "No, either you can or you can't." The air seemed too thick to breathe.

Amareth arched a brow. "We can," she said stiffly.

"Good." Relief washed over her but left her feeling empty. She felt nothing but the crushing pain that seemed to grow bigger by the minute. Without looking back she turned to walk out of the room when Mac caught her by the arm and spun her around to face him.

"Running away? I didn't expect that, Legs." His body tensed as he baited her. The torment was there in his piercing green eyes.

"Well, make up your mind, MacDougal. Do you want me sequestered in my room or what?" The pain was too bright. It was getting too damn hard to hold back the tears.

Piercing emerald eyes searched hers as his thumb brushed away a tear she hadn't realized escaped. He lowered his head 'til his mouth was nearly touching her own. "Amareth, go away."

He was going to devour her. Mac jerked Elyiana against him, the hunger and the pain, the need and the desire exploding in him with a desperation he could no longer contain. He needed her. Needed her to soothe the white-hot fire of his passion, the dark, swirling mass of agony. He wasn't real, but this was. This passion, this need for her. This emotion that ripped through, the feeling of helplessness that he so abhorred and filled him with strength. She filled him with life, a life he hadn't known even before this mess.

"God, how beautiful you are," he whispered as he held her to him, feeling, seeing the fires of need and emotion swirling in her violet eyes. "You make me weak and strong in the same breath, Elyiana. You make me want all the things I know can never be mine."

His life wasn't one that he would wish on anyone so gentle, so perfect in mind and soul. She was everything he knew was good and beautiful in the world. And he knew he risked destroying that, risked the very things he loved about her if he ever tried to hold her to him.

"Mac." His name was a breathless cry and it speared straight to his nonexistent heart.

His hand rose, his palm cupping her cheek as he watched it cover her flesh. He could feel her, warm and alive. Like soft, living satin beneath his touch.

"I'll no take you wi' this body, ever again," he growled. "It's no my body. No me touching you, holding you. I'll no take you like this."

Her lips trembled as his thumb smoothed over them. They were like satin heat beneath his touch, calling to him, a silent plea for more.

"It's not the body that matters," she whispered then. "What's inside is what matters, Mac. And I lo—"

"No." He stopped the words. He couldn't bear to hear them, not now, not when so much was so uncertain.

"Mac." Her breath hitched on a tearful cry as she stared up at him, tears swimming in a gaze that should be filled with laughter, not the pain he saw in them now.

He would have cried himself if it were possible. He could feel the emotion swelling within him, the bleak agony unlike anything he had ever known before and wished he could shed tears for all he had never known until now.

This was why he had been so desperate to get to her when his own mind had been in such chaos. Through her writings, the few emails and the single phone call to blast her for her romanticism, she had woven her way into his heart. He hadn't even realized it. How had he not realized how much she filled him, how much her words affected him?

Perhaps he had. Perhaps that was why he had been so determined to face her. He had wanted to touch her, to taste the wild passion he had only read about and scoffed at even then. He had wanted to feel the warmth of her spirit, the taste of her desire. And he had. Many times. And yet he hadn't.

He stared at his hand once again. Only the spirit of who and what he was touched her. He wasn't touching her. It wasn't his hand experiencing the softness of her flesh, his lips tasting her kiss, or his cock driving her to screaming orgasm.

"Go," he growled, jerking away from her.

He couldn't bear to continue touching her in such a way, couldn't bear the thought that his last kiss from her, the last stroke of his fingers against her flesh would be with a body not his own.

"Mac, it's still you." He could hear the tears in her voice as he turned his back to her. "No matter what, it's still you."

"No, Legs," he said wearily. "It's not me."

He looked at the stasis unit holding his still and silent body. Was that even him?

He shook his head at the regret simmering so deep inside his soul. He had spent a lifetime searching for revenge, and what had he gained? More blood, more death and betrayal. And the dreams, the desires that had once fed his soul had been pushed back, smothered by the drive to succeed and to avenge himself.

No, even that near-broken body, absent of his spirit, wasn't truly him. Mac was the man who had laughed to the vibrant wit of the woman standing behind him. Mac was the man who had loved her, had craved her, the man who had watched and listened in amazement to the dreams that drove her.

"I don't want to leave you alone." Her voice was thick with her tears, with emotion. "You drew me into this, Mac. You made me care. Don't push me away now."

He pushed his fingers through his long hair before crossing his arms over his chest, holding himself still and tense to keep from reaching out to her.

"Go to Amareth," he said tightly. "It will all be over soon, Legs, and then you can return to your life...and to your dreams."

And he would devour them, word by word, in each book she wrote. When it was over, what use would she have for The MacDougal, a man with blood on his hands and vengeance in his soul?

"Coward!" She accused him roughly then, her voice vibrating with anger and pain.

He turned to her, spearing her with his gaze as she stood trembling before him. Her hair framed her face, shades of platinum, black and purple that should have looked ridiculous, but on her, seemed entirely natural.

She was like one of those fairies his mother had once read him stories of. A fey magical creature that brought beauty and life in her wake.

"Och aye," he breathed then. "That I am, Legs. A coward. Because I know the man I am, and the woman you are, and I fear that as bad as your opinion of The MacDougal may be, the truth is far worse. A truth perhaps neither of us can fully accept."

"And I'm afraid you're so full of shit it's not even funny," she snapped back, surprising him. Infuriating him.

He arched a brow, pulling himself back, restraining the impulse to jerk her into his arms and to show her exactly how The MacDougal dealt with such mouthy women. A grin almost curled his lips at that thought. She reminded him of his own misplaced arrogance and his faults as no other person could. She reminded him of all he had thrown away in his life, and now may never have a chance at again.

"Don't lift that damned brow like that at me," she snorted, her lips thinning with displeasure. "With you, Mac, the body would never matter; you're always going to be an arrogant arse."

He did grin at that. He couldn't help it. She stood there, her hands on her hips; her eyes snapping violet fire, her face flushed with her anger and her passion and tore into him as though she had no reason to fear him, no need to be wary.

Others would have been trembling in fear of his fury, but not Elyiana, his Legs. She knew him as no other did, and he had forgotten that.

"Elyiana…" He whispered her name, intending to say so much more than he knew was wise. Salvation came in the form of Amareth's knock at the door before she entered quickly.

"Mac, we need to get started." There was no apology in her tone, but her gaze was filled with remorse. "The team is ready. We have to do this now."

He continued to watch Elyiana.

"And he's more than ready for you," she snorted with no small amount of feminine disdain. "See if you can't lose The MacDougal part of him somewhere and just bring back Mac. At least you can deal with him."

She turned and swept quickly from the room, her head held high, her body vibrating with her anger.

"Are you going to be foolish enough to lose her?" Amareth asked as Elyiana slammed the door behind her.

Mac turned a dark look on her. "Were you smart enough to take what you held?" he asked her.

She grimaced tightly. "Maybe I need someone to show me how to do it," she suggested before indicating the gurney at the side of the room. "Let's get you hooked up and get this done. And pray to God you can remember how you did it the first time."

Chapter Nineteen

"There was a blip on the transference screen when you managed to possess the droid," Amareth reported as he sat down on the gurney, facing her, watching her closely. "I am going to assume, from the reports and diagnostics we've run so far, that you knew you were dying." She paused and he watched as she swallowed tightly but her expression never changed. She was calm, composed.

"I was dyin', Am," he said softly. "We both knew it."

Eyes so like his own stared back at him before she looked away. "It's been a long time since you've called me Am," she whispered then. "With the brogue..." She shook her head, clearing her throat as her hands lifted to his head. "The computer outlets are hidden at the back of the neck. This model was designed to simulate a human male as closely as possible, so we hid the plate that opens to the computerized brain."

She lifted his hair and Mac admitted silently it was highly uncomfortable sensation, the feel of the back of his head opening.

"You know I would never tell your secrets, don't you, Am?"

There were things he needed to say before they took him under, before there was no chance left to say them.

She paused, her gaze flickering to his for a moment before she moved behind him.

"I know you wouldn't," she finally agreed coolly, though her voice held a trust that he wondered if he deserved.

He felt the sudden sensation of something clicking into place and winced. Damn he hated this.

"Am." He stopped her as she moved back to the row of computers in front of them.

She turned to face him, her green eyes darker, her gaze a bit moist. He had always taught her to hide her emotions, even from him. She was doing just that.

"Have I ever told you how proud I am of you?" he asked her then, tilting his head as he watched her.

She shrugged her shoulders uncomfortably. "I knew you were, or I wouldn't be here," she finally said confidently.

"Och, that's true," he sighed, nodding. "But Am, have I ever told you I was wrong?"

That made her pause. She stared back at him, a sudden flash of pain in her eyes as she watched him.

"Wrong about what?" She turned back to the monitors, pushing in several commands before pausing and turning back to him when he hadn't answered.

"I love you, Am," he said then, reaching out to touch her suddenly pale cheek. "I was wrong to never tell you this, to think that you should know it, rather than knowing I should show it. I was wrong to teach you to hold back, even from those of us who love you most. I was wrong, and if I don't see tomorrow, I want you to promise me you'll talk to Tael. Promise me you'll give him a chance to know the truth of your secrets."

Her breath hitched as she turned quickly from him, shaking her head roughly.

"You were right, Mac," she snapped painfully, and he knew it was pain, it throbbed in her voice, tightened every line of her body and it shamed him that he had never faced the pain his sister lived with.

"No, Am," he sighed. "I wasn't right. You can be strong and love as well. You can shed a tear when it hurts and still do what needs to be done. And you can regret, Am, the necessity of it, just as I regret now. I should have sheltered you, rather than raising you amid the demons I knew we faced. I could have protected you without making you bloody your hands. And barring that, I could have at least shown you a measure of love rather than forgetting myself what we're all fighting for."

"Stop." She gripped the edge of the counter with a desperation that broke his heart. "You did what you had to. You protected us. Raised us to survive..."

"But did I raise you to know love?" he asked her gently. "You've never told him. Even now, nearly five years later, you've never told Tael the truth, never told him of that night or its consequences to you. And you never let him close, even though I saw his longing to be close to you."

"It's lust," she snapped. "That's all it was. You agreed that was all it was."

"And how am I to know another man's heart?" he questioned her regretfully. "I knew your pain. I knew the cries I heard from your room deep in the night and the nightmares that haunted you. And I knew I couldn't protect you. All I could do was encourage you to bury it as I buried my own pain."

His voice was rising. He knew it, knew the emotion that throbbed inside him bared him to the sister he had always fought to hide emotion from.

He had hid it to teach her how. To show her the way of locking back the bitterness and the pain. And that was his greatest sin.

She turned to him then, her face twisting with the effort to hold back, her eyes glittering with tears she hadn't shed in five long years.

"I can't tell him," she whispered.

"That is your decision," he said, his voice softer, but lined with regret. "But know, Am, that I was wrong. Hiding your hurt, your love, hiding the parts of you that torment you in the deepest hours of the night will bring you no ease. I've learned this just this day," he admitted. "I see my sins and I know them for what they are. And I regret to the point that if I could go back, then I would do it differently. Much differently, Am."

"What's happened to you?" she snarled furiously then. "This isn't you, Mac. Something's gone wrong…"

He moved to keep her from jumping away from him, his hands gripping hers as he pulled her back to him, staring down at her now, restraining the urge to shake her, but knowing this was his fault. This was what he had taught her.

"I learned my weakness," he snapped. "When my memories were scrambled, my life a jumble of nothing more than impressions, I sought one thing, Am. I sought another's dreams, another's heart. I read her damned books and I hated her for what she showed me. Hated her to the point that I nearly broke that publishing company, and her, because she showed me all that I had turned my back on. But broken as I was, drifting and alone, it was her I ran to. Her dreams I took as my own. Do you not see, girl? I loved her before I even went to her. I love her and I hated her for it, because I saw in those damned books what she could give me, what I had cut myself from.

"She used me, Am, to create these men she wrote of, and in her heroines, she used herself, I see that now. Because I see her heart, and she showed me mine. Do you see? I was wrong, and God help me, I may never have another chance to tell you what I wouldn't accept myself until the choice was taken from me. I was wrong, Am, because I refused to love. And now, I may never have the chance to make up for that one sin alone. The most blinding, unforgivable sin imagined. I forgot how to love."

"I'll make it right," she cried out, beseeching, pleading. "I swear, Mac, I'll bring you back."

He lifted his hand, touching her hair, then her cheek.

"If you don't, then it's no because you failed," he said tenderly. "I did, Am. I failed. Long before now. I want you to always remember that. This is no your fault. And I'll no have you accepting blame for it if all goes wrong. This is no your sin, Am."

"Mac..." A single tear fell from her eyes, trailing slowly down her pale cheek.

He wiped the moisture away, staring at it for long pain-filled seconds.

"It's okay to cry," he said then, staring at the tear, wishing he could shed his own. "Remember that, Am. It's okay to cry."

It's okay to cry. Mac stared silently up at the ceiling of the lab as Amareth stood beside the gurney.

"It takes twelve hours to defrag the computer's brain," she said hoarsely. "As soon as it completes we'll begin the transference. I believe you felt something, somehow knew there was an escape from death. During defrag you'll be cognizant. See if you can remember what that was. What impression, impulse or whatever led you out of your body into the droid. That's the path you'll have to take back to your own body."

"I'll find the path, Am," he assured her. "I promise."

At least, he hoped he would.

"You won't be able to move or to speak," she continued. "I'm not certain how aware you'll be of what's going on around you but I assume it will rather be like sleeping. That's how we programmed the droid for this phase anyway. You'll have to be certain to let us know how it works."

"I'll be sure ta do that," he drawled a bit mockingly.

Silence met his words. Finally, he looked up at her rather than the ceiling.

"I always knew you loved me," she said then. "I always knew you did what you had to in protecting Jaime and I. I have no regrets, Mac, in the person you made me."

But he had many.

"You're a fine woman, Amareth MacDougal," he told her sincerely. "One of the finest I know. Now get to work and know no matter what happens, we all did our best."

She breathed out roughly before turning away, regret lingering in her gaze. A second later his strength left him with a flip of the switch and he watched as, quite literally, his own life began to flash before his eyes.

Chapter Twenty

Defragmenting was an uncomfortable procedure not because of the static, electrified sensations rushing through his brain, but because of the memories, long forgotten, that flashed past his inner vision. Memories of his parents, his life before their death. The promise he made to always protect Amareth and Jaime, then so very young.

His mother had cried. He remembered hearing her sobs as they killed his father, her ragged voice as she repeated his name over and over again before the final shot that took her life as well.

He remembered the illness from his own wounds, his regret and the pain that he had been unable to save them. He hadn't been strong enough, and he had cursed himself for that weakness.

He saw the events flashing past him, the years after, how he raised and trained Amareth, teaching her to be hard, to be strong, in case anything happened to him. She had to be strong, had to care for Jaime until he was grown. She would have to protect their holdings and their power and she had to learn that she could trust no one in doing that.

If he had a heart, it would have broken as he watched the young woman, once so filled with laughter, become a quiet, determined adult willing to kill to protect what she loved. But she did love. He held that close. He knew she loved.

The process was a long one, and patience wasn't once of his virtues. Unfortunately, sleeping through it wasn't an option, he was completely cognizant through the whole thing.

As the process began its final countdown to transference, Mac became aware of the lab doors opening. Helpless, unable to move, to see who the intruder was, he could only listen as the steps advanced toward him. Dammit it all, where were the guards that were supposed to be guarding the door? Where was Amareth?

"You should have died that night, MacDougal." Shock resounded through his system as he heard the voice. "It would have been better for all of us if you had died then."

Benjamin. Ben was a MacDougal, one of the younger men who had escaped the massacre of the family so long before.

"I'm tired of arranging your death for you, Mac," he sneered, his voice rougher, nothing like the smooth, amicable man Mac knew. "You and that bitch sister of yours should have died with your parents years ago instead of putting me out like this. You're going to pay for making me take these chances, Mac."

Ten seconds to transference… The computer's voice inside his head was a distant sound as he fought to move, to protect himself. His body was motionless, the sensors connecting his mind to the droid's neural system disconnected. He was a dead man.

"At least it won't be so messy this time…" he continued. "Robots don't bleed, do they, my man?" he snickered. "They just fuck stupid little authors who will have to follow you pretty quickly. I'll have almost as much fun killing her as I will killing you."

A shift of cloth, the sound of a satisfied sigh.

"Maybe I'll fuck her to death," he mused. "That would be so nice, if I could stomach your seconds. I've grown damned tired of those, Mac."

Five seconds to transference…

Mac concentrated on the electrical impulses building in his mind. There was only one escape. Only one way out and he knew it.

"Do you know what a lazer pistol can do to electronics, Mac?" Ben crooned, amusement and merciless pleasure echoing in his voice.

He was going to rip his fucking head off. Fury swelled inside him.

Four seconds to transference…

He could feel the surging power in his head, an electrical field wrapping around it, like the static buzz of a million bees working in tandem.

"Get ready, MacDougal. Dirty bastard that you are. Here's where you pay…"

Three seconds to transference…

Fury overwhelmed him, consumed him as he heard the lazer power up, felt the sense of his own death, more powerful now than it had been before.

"I might die with you, but I'll know it will be my son carrying on Mac. Not your bitch sister or that mongrel brother or yours. Because they'll go next. They'll die, Mac, just as you will. Just as your pretty little author will."

Transference beginning…

Mac threw everything he had into following the sudden surge of energy, his spirit rushing to escape. Nothing mattered but escape, but surviving, living… His silent growl of fury was followed by the sound of the lazer firing, the weapon discharging into the computer before everything went black…

His eyes flew open. His eyes. His body. Weak, but alive, strong enough to instantly process the fact that Ben was turning for the opened stasis unit, shock on his face as he saw Mac staring back at him.

His finger tightened on the lazer's trigger. Throwing himself to the side, Mac landed on the cold hard floor a second before sparks flew around him, the electronics within the unit reacting to the energy blast shot into it. Alarms were blaring, the sound of imperative screams coming closer.

"You bastard!" Ben screamed out in crazed fury as another blast hit only feet from Mac as he rolled for the questionable safety of the bank of computers that controlled the life support unit.

Seconds later, sparks rained around him again as he threw himself at a low run toward Ben's unprotected legs. They went down, shattered curses filling the melee of sound as the door to the lab crashed open.

Chaos was a mild term for the shouted voices, the crush of bodies and the struggle to make sense of who was in the tangle of violence rushing around him. He managed one hard blow to Ben's testicles, rendering him useless before he came to his knees, his fist pulled back to land another on whoever dared to be coming behind him.

"Mac…" Jaime stared back at him, his dark green eyes wide, horrified in his pale face as his gaze swung to the fist then back to his face. "Mac, it's okay, man. You took him down. We have him now."

They had him. His head swung around to see the guards jerking Ben to his feet, his lanky body bent as he heaved for breath. Amareth moved in front of him, her lazer gun aiming for the other man's head.

"No," Mac gasped, struggling to reach her. "Stop, Am…"

He struggled to his feet, pushing Jaime's helping hand aside, determined to stand on his own two feet, as weak as they were.

Amareth turned back to him, her eyes wide, filled with her own anger.

"He tried to kill you, not once but twice," she snapped, eyes blazing. "Do you think his death is going to matter to me?"

"It will to me," he lifted his arm, his fingers gripping the hand holding the weapon. "It will matter to me, Am. Lock him up. He's not working alone and we need that information. We'll deal with the rest…" He wavered on his feet, grimacing a bit with self-mockery. "When I can stand alone."

He would have fallen if it weren't for Jaime and the guards behind him.

"Get him into the extra unit," Amareth snapped. "And lock this bastard up." She waved at her cousin carelessly.

The extra unit was wheeled in place, minus the computers that were still sparking on the other side of the room. Mac laid back in it gratefully, thankful to get off his shaky legs.

"Where's Ellie?" He needed to see her. To know she was safe as well.

"She's safe, Mac," she breathed out roughly. "She's in her room resting and safe. I made certain of it."

He breathed in, exhausted, amazed at the weakness of his own body. But damned glad to be in it once again.

"How much longer before this is over?" he snarled. "This weakness is a bitch."

"Another twelve hours in stasis, no less," the doctor snapped. "Or you can leave early and risk more serious health issues. I give up with you two. There's nothing more that I can do. The unit does the rest."

He nodded slowly. "Am, you go to Elyiana and stay with her every second. Don't leave her for a moment. Jaime and Tael will stay in here with me and your head doctor. I want the labs closed down and this room sealed closed. No entry, no exit without my code as well."

He was aware of Tael moving to do that before he ever issued the command. Confident that at least no one could get in, he lay back and allowed his eyes to close wearily. How long since he had slept? Rested? He couldn't remember the last time.

"We'll take care of it," she promised. "Sleep, Mac," Amareth's voice was husky, filled with regret. "Rest now."

He closed his eyes and did just that.

Chapter Twenty-One

The door slid open and Elyiana stood bracing herself. Scott stood behind her rubbing her shoulders, trying to be supportive. Hours had gone by, mere hours that seemed more like days. If he was gone, her Mac was dead she wasn't sure she could cope with it. With her heart in her throat, she faced Amareth.

"The transference was successful," Amareth said tightly. Elyiana breathed a sigh of relief. Had she been breathing at all? "The mole has been caught as well and he's locked up. To be dealt with soon."

The mole? Elyiana just stared at her for a moment before asking. "How did that happen?"

"It was our cousin; he was in the lab at the time of transference and tried to kill Mac, again. He was unsuccessful. As a matter of fact he probably aided in its success. Mac woke and took him down until we were able to get to him," Amareth explained.

Elyiana grappled for understanding, noting the rage in Amareth's eyes; her body was rigid with it. "But Mac is okay? Was he hurt?" Her own body ached from the tension, the worry that the transference wouldn't work. Learning of another attempt on his life infuriated her.

Amareth shook her head "No, he wasn't hurt, Mac is fine. It's imperative that he remain in stasis for a while longer. He's still weak. But he will recover completely."

"Oh, good." She'd prayed the whole time, pleading, begging and finally bargaining with God that He'd just let Mac be okay. Silently she thanked Him for answering her.

"Is this bastard cousin of yours dead?" Elyiana asked gruffly.

"Unfortunately no. Mac wouldn't let me kill him," Amareth grumbled.

"But he won't get away with it?" she asked pointedly. "I can trust you to make him pay. Can't I?"

A feral smile curved Amareth's lips. "No, he won't get away with it and yes, he will pay. Absolutely, you have my word."

Tamping down on her anger, Elyiana nodded, satisfied that Amareth would deal with the man justly. Although she would rather he be dead after what he did to Mac, The MacDougal. Dear God. Would all of this ever make sense? Probably not, she answered herself silently. The best thing to do at this point was to get home. Where she could heal. Taking a deep breath, she asked "So is it safe for us to go home now?"

Amareth frowned and crossed her arms. "Yes, it's safe. But don't you want to wait 'til Mac awakens?"

Elyiana swallowed hard and looked down at her hands as the pain pulsed through her with every heartbeat. Yes, yes she wanted to see him. But he didn't want her, didn't want her love. Not now, not anymore. "No, no I think it's best we leave as soon as possible." Looking up she met Amareth's hard gaze. "I wanted to know he's safe. I'm so thankful he's safe." The MacDougal detested her, couldn't stand her. Remembering the contempt The MacDougal held for her, the disgusted expression on his face when he'd called, fresh pain bloomed in her chest. He'd have no use for her. The realization of it was gut-wrenching.

"Can I change your mind? Mac will want to see you." Amareth's voice softened, her face began to blur as the tears filled Elyiana's eyes.

"It will all be over soon, Legs, and then you can return to your life…and to your dreams." No, he wouldn't want to see her. He'd turned his back on her, told her to go. Mac was lost to her forever now. Shaking her head she took another deep breath as she flicked away the errant tears. "No, no, I want to go as soon as possible."

"If that's what you want, I won't keep you here against your will," Amareth said. "I'll go make the arrangements." Stopping at the door she turned back to Elyiana. "If you reconsider, let me know. You're welcome to stay as long as you wish."

"Amareth?"

"Yes?"

"Do you know what…ghraw mo cry ah, what does that mean?

Amareth's brows knit together, then her eyes widened. "Do you mean *Ghrá mo cridhe*?"

"Yes, that's it."

Amareth stared at her for a moment then answered. "It means, *love of my heart*."

A spark of hope glimmered in her heart, warm and bright before she quickly doused it. No, it had only been a dream, she told herself. Not real, in reality he'd turned his back on her. What a powerful thing an imagination can be. Unconscious desires had a way of making themselves known. He didn't love her. She would not wait around for him to reject her again.

Clearing her tight throat she met Amareth's gaze. "Thank you," she said with finality, hoping Amareth would just leave before she collapsed in a blubbering heap of anguish.

"You're welcome," Amareth said softly as the door slid shut behind her.

Her heart was breaking but she knew she was doing the right thing. She couldn't stand to see the cold contempt in the eyes of The MacDougal. Not now. Scott held her as she sobbed into her hands.

"Look, love, why not go to him. Tell him you love him," Scott said, rubbing her arm. *Tried that,* she thought, *didn't go over well.* "If he turns you away, I'll beat his sorry arse to a pulp." At Elyiana's snort, he stiffened. "Well, he isn't a blasted machine now. I could probably take him."

"Yeah, you could Scott. But I don't want either of you hurt. He doesn't want to hear my declaration of love. It wouldn't change anything. I don't want to hurt anymore either."

Scott pulled her closer. She laid her head on his shoulder and cried softly. "Go ahead and let it out, love. I'll be here for you."

"Everything was fine, Scott. I was happy with my life the way it was. Why did he have to come around and blast it all to hell?"

"I don't know, babe. I'm so sorry," he said, kissing the top of her head. "Ellie, let's wait. Talk to him."

She shook her head. "No! I can't. Don't you see Scott? He never wanted me. He wasn't himself. He was a bloody sex droid. Everything that happened between us only happened because he wasn't aware. The MacDougal isn't

Mac. My Mac is lost forever now. He was never real in the first place."

Scott lifted her chin with a finger and met her gaze. "This time I think you're wrong, Ellie."

"No, Scott. I'm not and I want to go home," she said firmly. In time her heart would heal. It had when her parents died…mostly. It would heal again. But the loss now was devastating and she felt empty. She needed to get home, surround herself with the things that she was familiar with and try to let go of the one and only man she'd ever loved.

"Then we'll go home," he said with a sigh, pulling her head back down onto his shoulder.

Chapter Twenty-Two

She was gone. Mac stood in the middle of the room she had inhabited, Amareth silent behind him, and stared at the neatly made up bed.

"Mac, I couldn't force her to stay. If I had…"

"I don't blame you." And he didn't. He allowed the blame to fall squarely on his own shoulders.

Amareth had disobeyed his direct order for the first time in their lives. But she respected Ellie, and Mac knew there were damned few people besides him, that Amareth truly liked or respected. She wouldn't have forced Elyiana to stay unless her life was in direct danger. The information they had gleaned from Ben's interrogation indicated it wasn't.

He wouldn't let her whisper her words of love, wouldn't allow her the promises she needed at the time. He couldn't. Not then. The lack of them would have fueled her need to run, to distance herself from further rejection. His Elyiana wouldn't stay where she felt she wouldn't be wanted. The problem was, she wasn't just wanted, she was required. He needed her to survive the morass of emotions and hunger let free now. She was his woman. He wouldn't let her escape.

"Is my glider ready?" He turned toward her, seeing the indecision on her face.

"Mac, give her time…"

"Amareth, now's not a good time ta be pissin' me off," he drawled coldly. "You let her leave, and I understand the why of it. But that's my woman, and I'll be damned if I'll let her escape me so easily."

Behind her, Tael crossed his arms over his chest, staring back at Mac broodingly.

"Your glider's ready. I took care of it myself," he said firmly. "Me and two of our best wingmen will accompany you. We're not out of the woods yet with this conspiracy against the family, Mac. Allow us to protect you at least."

Mac nodded sharply. He had learned the value of allowing his bodyguards to do their job with the attack that had precipitated his time spent inside a body not his own.

"That wasn't your place," Amareth hissed when she turned on Tael furiously. "You are overstepping your bounds, McLeod."

He snorted sarcastically. "I wondered when you would realize that." He raised his gaze to Mac. "I have two men who followed her and her friend back to her home and set up watch there. We'll meet with them when we arrive."

Amareth hissed furiously at the information. Her gaze flashing to Tael with a promise of retribution.

"There was no danger to her. I wouldn't have let her leave if there was."

"That's not the point," Tael said mockingly. "My job is to clear the way for The MacDougal, Amareth. You're head of security and second-in-command, but I'm your fucking ghost. Remember that one. And my job is to make certain I anticipate things like this."

"Asshole patrol," she snapped, but Mac saw the fear in her eyes as she glanced away from the other man.

"Beats the Bitch Brigade." He shrugged nonchalantly. "Get used to it."

Mac smiled tightly at their byplay, though he was in no way amused enough to forget his fury. He was going to break every bone in Scott Forester's body when he got there just because he was with her. Was he comforting her? Holding her? Shrugging his shoulders beneath the expensive silk shirt he wore, Mac moved for the door.

He was slowly getting used to his own body again. He wasn't super-strong anymore, but he wasn't weak either. He was as tall, as well-honed as the droid, but the similarity stopped there. His hair was much shorter, barely brushing the collar of his shirt, and darker than it had been in his younger days. His body was scarred, his nose still showed the untended break from years before, and he could feel his own sense of mortality now.

"Mac, give her time." Amareth gripped his forearm as he started pass her. "She needs to come to grips with everything that's happened."

He stared down at his sister, seeing the swirling shadows of fear in her gaze then. Shadows he had never noticed before.

"No, Am," he denied her request. "I'll give her no time to build her defenses against me. No time for her to find reasons why this cannot be. She's mine, and I'll not be fool enough to let her go."

"It's her choice as well, Mac. You can't force her." She kept her voice low, because of Tael, he knew. If there was one person on the face of the Earth that she wanted to never show a weakness to, then it was Tael.

"There will be no force," he assured her. "None will be needed. While I'm gone, I want the castle prepared for my arrival. There's going to be a wedding there, Am, and laughter and joy is going to fill the empty husk of those halls or it's going to come down, brick by damned brick." His ancestral home was haunted by the screams of his mother and the pain that had ripped through the MacDougal and McLeod families so long before.

Amareth stepped back slowly.

"And if it's not what she wants?" she asked him then.

"Then she best be deciding otherwise," he growled. "Because I'll be damned if I'll let her run."

There was nothing more to say in that regard.

"Let's fly, Tael." He strode quickly from the room, followed by Tael and several other guards as he made his way to the opposite end of the main labs.

"The coordinates are already programmed into the gliders," Tael reported. "I knew we'd be heading there."

"I want the security force put on high alert once we arrive," Mac snapped. "I don't know what the hell is going on here, Tael, but I'll not have my family, any of them, endangered again. Is that understood?"

"Understood."

And Mac knew it was. Tael took security more seriously than Amareth had ever given him credit for.

"Let's get in the air then," he bit out. "I'm tired of waiting."

More than twelve hours in the stasis unit and then another four regaining his strength was sixteen hours too long to wait as far as he was concerned. If he had known Elyiana would run like this, he would have given the order to lock her in and keep her there. But he had thought she would stay. In his arrogance, he had believed she would be there, waiting for him. He had forgotten that Elyiana was stronger than that. That she would refuse to wait on a man who couldn't accept her love, let alone reveal his own.

The flight to Australia was accomplished in record time. There was no time to waste as far as he was concerned. They landed in the front yard of Elyiana's home as clouds rolled in from the ocean, darkening the land around them in threat of the coming storm.

"Pull everyone back from the house," he snapped into the microphone attached to his ear. "I want no one within sight after Forester leaves the premises."

"He left an hour ago, Mr. MacDougal," one of the security guard's answered. "She sent him off with a kiss on the cheek and a cheery little wave."

There was a thread of amusement in the guard's voice.

"Damned good thing," he muttered. "I'd hate to have to kill him in front of her."

Though he knew he wouldn't. He knew that Elyiana wouldn't have attempted to touch the other man, nor allowed him to touch her. If there was one thing that came through about her in her books, it was her sense of commitment, her belief in loyalty and fidelity. Her heart belonged to him now; she wouldn't betray that.

He jumped from his glider as the others lifted off and moved beyond the line of sight of the house. It was a move Tael hadn't been happy with when Mac had discussed it with him earlier, but it was one he would live with. Every precaution had been taken to make certain the area was secure and that it could be monitored for anyone other than himself and Elyiana.

"Legs, open this fucking door." He didn't bother to knock when he reach the wood panel. He knew she was waiting, listening.

He was right. The door flew open to reveal an enraged she-cat ready to rip his throat out.

"Get off my property," she ordered furiously. "If I wanted you here I would have sent you an invitation, MacDougal."

The sneering contempt in her voice set his teeth on edge.

"Mac," he snarled. "My name is Mac."

"You're The MacDougal," she sneered. "You proved that at those damned labs. Confine her to her rooms," she mocked, throwing his words back at him. "You belong to me, Elyiana," she further pushed his patience with her sarcasm. "You are so full of crap, you arrogant, superior son of a—"

He would be damned if he could bear to listen to her fury, her pain, another second. Before he knew what he intended, he was jerking her forward, his lips covering hers, stilling the angry outburst as hunger began to overwhelm him in overriding waves.

God help him, she tasted better than he had thought. Her skin was softer, her lips cushioning his better, her gasp of surprise and shock a stroke to his senses unlike anything he had ever known.

Amareth was wrong. The Battery Operated Boyfriend she had created was in no way superior to a male's sense of perception. He could taste Elyiana like the most addictive wine, sweet and potent, her passion whipping through his system with an elemental fury that had nothing on the storm suddenly breaking around them.

But the storm fueled something inside him he hadn't known existed. Without taking his lips from her, hearing her moan echo in the winds whipping around them, he lifted her against him, moving her into the dampness falling on the land.

Rain quickly saturated his clothing and her thin dress. The dark colors became a shadow on her body as her legs gripped his hips, her hands tearing at his shirt. Hunger, primal, fierce, built inside them, singing through his veins and setting his heart to racing.

She was the storm. She was the wind. The lightning and the rain. She was as heady as the storm, as enduring as the land around them.

"I love you, Legs," he groaned as he felt his shirt part beneath her hands, felt her lips at his neck as he nipped at her ear. "With my soul, with all that I am and could ever be, I love you, woman..."

Chapter Twenty-Three

It was nothing like anything she'd ever known, this hunger, this need to be a part of him. Thunder shook her world as his words struck her heart. Lifting her head she searched his eyes. "Mac?" The sound of her voice was swallowed by the storm. Blinking back the tears, the rain that pelted her face, her fingers traced the scar on his cheek. Everything seemed to shift into place.

"Elyiana mine, I love you." It was a declaration, a promise. Unmistakable.

"I love you." She wasn't sure if she actually spoke the words or just mouthed them. Mac kissed her roughly chasing away everything but the feel of him. His lips slid over hers, his tongue stroked the delicate interior of her mouth. The taste of him intoxicated her. How had she missed the taste of him? Inhaling deeply, she'd never get enough his scent. Clean, spicy, male, it made her ravenous for him.

With a growl he bared his teeth as he ripped her panties from her, tossing the ruined scrap of silky material aside. White-hot and frenzied, their desire was like a living thing demanding satisfaction. His fingers found her, stroking her he spread her open, entered her. Moisture pooled, flowed from her, bathing his hand as she moaned, riding his fingers.

Ragged breath shuddered from him as his chest rose and fell beneath her palm. The hair on his chest, the scars, this was him, really him. Trembling against him, she struggled to get closer to his body, his skin. His mouth was hot, voracious and she tilted her head back on a whimper to give him better access to her throat. The feel of him, her need for him, seemed amplified. Her hands tore at his clothes, fought with the button of his pants, his fly, as he withdrew his fingers, spreading her slick cream back to circle her tight rear opening.

Finally freeing his erection, she rose in his arms positioning the wide head of his cock at her entrance. A hiss escaped her as she lowered herself onto his thick staff. Clinging to him, she arched her back, his arm holding her as he worked his erection into the tight glove of her cunt. So hot, his shaft throbbed inside her, expanding the muscled walls, taking possession.

"Mine," he shouted huskily above the raging storm. Thrusting deeper still inside her as his finger circled and pressed firmly against her anus, demanding admittance.

"Yes," she answered weakly as she took him into her body, her heart.

Through her soaked dress his mouth closed over her nipple drawing it into his mouth, his tongue rasping over the tip. With a bite of pain, his finger entered her back hole, as his cock surged inside her. Intense pleasure stole her breath. Clenching her sheath around him drawing him in. It seemed as though she was aware of every tiny sensation. Every pulsing vein of his cock, the feel of his biceps bunching under her hand, the rough pleasure of his tongue on her nipples.

"So good, so perfect. God, I love you Ellie, my Ellie." Mac groaned as he surged into her, she arched to meet his thrusts.

Moving up and down on him, the crisp hair of his chest grazed her ultra-sensitive breasts adding another layer of sensations. Lightning flashed around them. Grasping her hips, he bared his teeth as he pistoned inside her. Thunder shook their world and for a moment she hovered breathless on the precipice of her climax, gripped in pure pleasure. Screaming, her nails bit into his flesh as she plummeted into the vortex of an orgasm so strong she thought it might tear her apart. Her pussy gripped him, convulsing around him as she soared upward again only to be thrown into another whirlwind of ecstasy.

It didn't take long for him to follow her. With a roar that drowned out her own weakening cries, his head fell back and he filled her, pumping hot jets of his seed into her. Milking him of every drop, her cunt convulsed around him greedily. Lifelessly she collapsed against him, her head against his chest.

The beat of his heart thudded strong and rapid in her ear. Tears mingled with the raindrops that slid down her cheeks as she kissed his chest. She hadn't even noticed that he'd carried her into the house until he sat her on the floor of her bathroom and pulled her drenched dress over her head.

Smoothing a hand over her shoulder he murmured, "Mmm, you're so soft." With both hands he cupped her breasts, lifting them, his thumbs grazing her nipples. "Beautiful. Mine."

God, how she wanted to believe this was real. That he really loved her. But he'd rejected her, turned his back on her. The moment he realized who he was, who she was he went hard, cold, locked her out. What made him come to her professing his love? Lifting her gaze to his, she couldn't help the tears. Her body trembled with residual ripples of pleasure. "Mac, why…"

"Because, I dinna know, Ellie. I dinna know if it would work. If I told you how I felt, if I had allowed you to say the words, they would have be out there for you to bear alone if I dinna come back to you," he explained as he took a towel from the shelf and began to dry her.

It amazed her how someone so intelligent could be so ignorant. "You hurt me Mac. You pushed me away. Had you died in transference, I would have had to bear the pain. Alone. Forever." She punched him in the stomach and winced at the jarring pain that radiated up her arm. He might not be a machine but he was still hard as a rock.

Stunned, he gazed down at her. His brows furrowed over stormy green eyes. He raised her fist to his lips. Pressing a kiss to her knuckles. "I couldna, love. Maybe it was the wrong thing. But I wanted to hear those words with my own ears. Touch you with my own hands."

His pain was a tangible thing. He'd been afraid, terrified. She could see that now. Something had changed in him while he was locked inside that machine replica of himself. Something broke, opened up inside him. His emotions had been set free. It would not be easy for him, learning to feel again. Facing the things that closed him off from love. Stepping forward, she wrapped her arms around his waist and held on. Closing her eyes, she listened to the steady rhythm of his heartbeat. "I could listen to your heart for the rest of my life. It sounds so wonderful."

"Will you?" he asked huskily, his hand smoothing over her hair.

Waiting for him to finish his question, she tensed. Forgive him? Yes. Let him go now? No. "Will I what?" she asked warily.

"Will you listen to my heart for the rest of your life?" His hands moved down her back as he pressed his growing erection against her quivering stomach.

Momentarily she froze then pulled away looking up into his face, afraid to ask what he meant by that. The corner of his mouth curved, his crystal sea green eyes sparkled with passion, with love.

"I'm askin' you to marry me, woman," he said gruffly.

She forgot to breathe. "I know," she said, absorbing the moment.

Large hands grasped her ass and pulled her against his unyielding body. "And?" He frowned, arching a brow.

"I'll marry you, MacDougal. On one condition," she said, growing serious.

"Anything."

Framing his face with her hands, his rough stubble felt good lightly scratching her palms. "You can never shut me out again, Mac. No matter what you feel, don't hide it from me. You can't deny me the right to share them with you. I love you, I will always love you. Promise me that."

With his thumb he wiped the tear from her cheek. "I promise, love. With all that is within me. I promise."

Epilogue

Three Weeks Later
Castle MacDougal, Scotland

"They're tucked securely at the castle," Jaime reported as he entered the makeshift security offices set on the outer perimeter of the MacDougal ancestral land. "They're fighting again, though. Damn, I've never heard Mac yell like that, Amareth. Do you think he'll hurt her?"

Amareth glanced up from the reports she held in her hand and stared at her younger brother silently for long minutes.

"He won't hurt her," she finally said confidently.

Mac was slowly changing, evolving in a way that confused and even sometimes saddened her. His time spent in the droid had been a time of revelations for him evidently. He was as strong as he had ever been, but he was more apt to smile now, and he had even hugged her the week before.

With Elyiana, he was a completely different man. He touched the woman often, was rarely far from her and seemed to luxuriate in her presence whether they were fighting or fucking. And they were prone to be doing either one or the other when in each other's presence.

"It's still damned strange," Jaime remarked as he stood beside the lazer-proof glass and stared up at the castle. "Makes it uncomfortable to be around them sometimes."

None of them were used to the intense emotion that reflected in Mac's eyes now. He was still a harsh taskmaster; that was too ingrained in him to ever change. But, he was no longer cold or unemotional. He no longer hoarded his affection for them, but gave it to them unselfishly. He showed his trust of them now, and Amareth hadn't realized how much she had needed that.

"Maybe they'll settle down in a few days." She lifted her shoulder as though it didn't matter. Truth be told, she was damned jealous. Suddenly, she was reminded of everything she didn't have herself.

For a moment, her heart stopped at the flash of memory. Usually she could hold it back, keep it from tormenting, but more and more lately it rose inside her like a destructive beast intent on shredding her alive.

"Open for me, Amareth..." Tael's voice, dark, slurred with the medication she had given him for his wounds. But neither those wounds, nor the pain, had stopped him that night.

He had held her beneath him, parting her thighs with a confidence, a determination that had left her gasping. Then he had pressed inside her, his cock thick and hot, forging his way inside the tight muscular walls of her vagina as she bucked and cried out beneath him.

She had climaxed on the first stoke, and it hadn't been her last orgasm. It hadn't been the only way he had taken her. He had demanded everything from her, and she had given it, reveled in it, relished it.

The next morning, he had awakened as she showered, groggy, the medication and the excesses of that night having left him drained. And he hadn't remembered. She had known as she stepped back into the room and saw his gaze swing to her, that he hadn't remembered. And she would have died before reminding him.

But his touch. She wanted to whimper at the remembered feel of it, the hunger it caused to rise inside her. His touch still affected her, made it impossible for her to forget.

"Tael's on his way in," Jaime reported then as he slouched down in the chair beside her.

She tensed at the information. She didn't need Tael there.

"Yeah, we need him here," she snorted. "Ghost, my arse. The man thinks he's indispensable."

She rose to her feet, nervous energy filling her at the knowledge that she was going to be stuck here with him.

"When is he due to arrive?" she finally snapped.

"Few more hours." Jaime leaned close to the bank of monitors, fiddling with the controls until he had a clearer view through the storm raging outside before relaxing back in his seat.

"I'll be resting in my room for a while. Let me know when he's ready to land."

Jaime grunted an affirmative as she turned and headed through the small stone house to her rooms in the back. She locked her door firmly before walking to the low dresser and pulling out the top drawer. There, innocuously, lay the small remote she had sworn she wouldn't use here.

She picked it up, pressed the activation switch and stood silently as the doors at her side slowly opened.

"Amareth." Smoky dark, his voice washed over her. "Come, love, I've been waiting on you."

Wide male hands settled on her shoulders, smoothing down her arms. His flesh was warm, calloused, stroking a response in her that was tinged with bitterness.

She allowed him to draw her to the bed, his hands stroking along her upper body as his lips and tongue tasted the skin at her neck.

"I've missed you," the hungry growl was nearly perfect. The way his teeth nipped at the lobe of her ear, the ripping of her shirt as he tore it from her body.

Her hands gripped the muscular forearms as she closed her eyes against the tears that would have fallen. It was almost perfection.

"Look at me, Amareth." He lifted her face, staring down at her with dark gray eyes slowly darkening with his passion.

His black hair fell over his wide brow, shaggy and disheveled from the night before.

"Hold me," she whispered, pushing back her rage over the pretension, allowing the fantasy to have her, but there was little else at this point to hold onto.

"I'll always hold ya, love." His brogue wasn't thick, but there all the same. "I'll hold ya forever."

The inflection of his voice didn't change, the emotion never wavered. A tear slid slowly down her cheek as she raised her head for his kiss. His lips settled over hers, warm, firm, his kiss dominant, demanding.

Amareth moaned at the touch, her breasts swelling as she allowed the fantasy to build in her mind, pushed back the lies, the deception she was practicing and allowed the heat and hardness of his body to sweep her away.

"Tael," she whispered his name on a sigh, one of hunger and need.

"Yes, lass, I have ya," he whispered as he unlaced her vest, revealing her swollen breasts to his dark gaze.

His hands cupped her slowly, his thumbs rasping over the distended peaks as her breath hitched in her throat. Yes, that was good, so good.

"Let's get you undressed, love," he whispered. "I want to see you naked before me, bare and ready for my touch. Do you remember my touch, Amareth? Do you remember how hot, hot wild it can get?"

She remembered. Oh God, how she remembered how hot and wild he was when he was taking her.

"Yes." Her moan was one of strangled carnal need as her hips tilted forward against the erection pressing at her lower stomach.

"Go wild for me then, Amareth," he whispered, his thumb and forefinger tweaking her nipple as his other hand tore at the laces of her pants, his hand slipping inside. "Wet and wild and hungry for me, baby. I'm going to make you scream as you come around my cock."

She whimpered. Yes, that was what she wanted, what she needed. Tael, hot and demanding, his cock thrusting inside her, making her scream in need. She followed the gentle nudge he gave her to recline on the bed, felt his hands sliding her pants from her legs, spreading her thighs.

"Yes, touch me," she moaned, her hands threading through his hair as she felt his tongue on her sensitive bare flesh, licking at the sweet juices that flowed from her pussy.

He moaned at the sound washing over her as she fell deeper, ever deeper into the touch and the need she so desperately craved.

He licked around her clit, suckled it slowly, destructively. His fingers parted the slick lips, one sliding between them to press into the empty recess of her vagina. Her muscles convulsed, clamping on the penetration as her hips jerked in response.

"Don't make me wait," she whispered, willing to beg.

She was so wet, so hot, so ready to be fucked she knew it would take no more than a few strokes to push her over the edge.

"You love the waiting," he whispered against the swollen knot of nerves he was caressing.

She did. She was demented. Perverse. Tael had made her wait for his possession that first night. He had made her scream, beg for him, had done things to her that she couldn't find the nerve to program the droid to do.

So her Tael licked and suckled instead. Gently, lovingly, he worked her flesh with expert skill until she was panting, sweating, ready to beg for her release as she felt it sweeping over her.

Then he was moving over her, pushing her legs up to enclose his hips as the head of his cock began to enter the moist, greedy depths of her pussy.

"Fuck me," she demanded, her eyes opening just enough to allow the hazy impression of his features through.

Tael, her Tael. Strong and bold, taking her again, loving her.

He thrust forward in one hard, blinding stroke, pulling a cry from her chest as she arched in his arms, the pleasure/pain of the penetration sending blinding streaks of sensation whipping through her body.

Yes! This was it. This was what she needed. She writhed beneath him, her thighs holding him tight as he began to pound hard and deep inside her, fucking her with an almost brutal pace as she felt her womb tightening in response.

"Harder." She needed more. Needed the fast blinding shards of sensation that would send her spiraling.

"Yes, lass, much harder." And he gave her harder, thrusting to the very depths of her pussy as her mouth opened on a soundless cry and her release exploded inside her with dizzying force.

"I love you," she whispered, a breath of sound, a prayer.

"I love you, lass." Programmed response. Her chest tightened in pain as he moved from her, drawing her further into the bed as he pulled her into his arms.

Programmed, but enough to allow a small balm to the needs building inside her. He wasn't her Tael, but he was close enough. Or was he?

Enjoy this excerpt from

Moving Violations

Chapter One

Jericho, Tennessee. The hick town still held so many bittersweet memories. Rebecca Taylor had only visited once since she'd left and she wouldn't be back now if Aunt Josie hadn't died. Rebecca frowned as she searched the cabinet for more plates. The house was full of people. Some she knew from her childhood, some she didn't know. Rebecca had few memories of her father's reclusive sister, but she knew she didn't have friends. She hardly ever left her house. Aunt Josie had been such a private woman. Rebecca never expected this many people would attend her funeral, much less come by the house to offer condolences.

She walked into the dining room and set the plates at the end of the highly polished mahogany table, looking it over. Covered dishes, casseroles and cakes were plentiful and there was one lone bucket of Kentucky Fried Chicken. She couldn't help but smile at that. The doorbell rang and Rebecca sighed. At least maybe with all these people all the food would be eaten. She'd hate to have to throw it away.

Rebecca made her way through the crowd occasionally nodding and saying, "Thank you," as folks laid sympathetic hands on her arm and whispered their condolences.

Finally she reached the door, swung it open and looked up into the face of Jackson Montgomery, her first love. It didn't matter that he was ten years older than her.

It didn't matter that he'd only seen her as a pesky little kid. Even when she was sixteen and her dad brought her along that summer to check on Aunt Josie.

He had been a Marine then, home on leave, and she had fancied herself in love. Her young body was blossoming and hormones were raging. She had flirted shamelessly and he'd teased her as usual. Still, it had been a powerful crush and the memories of those emotions had stayed with her through the years.

At the tender age of eleven her parents had yanked her roots and moved away from her quiet country hometown to the cold, often cruel city of Detroit. She'd been torn away from the only life she'd known, from friends she'd had since birth and grown up with, people she cared about and who cared about her. It had been painful for her, but what especially broke her young heart was leaving Jackson.

Now here he was again and that familiar tug low in her tummy was still there. He looked amazing in his black slacks and dark gray dress shirt. He took off his black Stetson and thick black hair fell across his forehead in spite of the good cut. There wasn't an inch of fat on that flat stomach. He had broader shoulders, leaner hips, and well-formed thighs with new bulges in all the right places. Rebecca let her eyes travel to his mouth and couldn't help but admire the way his full, well-defined lips contrasted with the hard planes and angles of his tan face.

Jackson had definitely changed; he'd gone from cute and sexy to hot and dangerous! "Jackson," she said with more composure than she felt. She mentally shook herself and stepped back from the door.

He stepped in, shutting the door behind him, never taking his intense gray eyes from hers. "I'm sorry I couldn't make it to the funeral but I wanted to come by to extend my condolences."

She couldn't find her voice so she just nodded and smiled tremulously.

He stepped closer and rubbed her bare upper arm. "How are ya holdin' up, Pixie?" His hand was warm, a little callused, and sent a sizzling electric current through her body. She crossed her arms over her chest to hopefully hide her tightening nipples. God, could he see what he did to her?

"I'm okay, Jackson, thank you," she croaked then cleared her throat. "Everyone brought food. The dining room table is overflowing. Help yourself."

He followed her through the living room to the dining room. She turned and almost jumped back. He was standing inches away looking down at her. His brows furrowed, his gaze sharply assessing her. She could smell him—warm, spicy male. She felt flushed with heat, awareness. She opened her mouth to say something but forgot what she wanted to say.

"Are you sure you're all right?" Jackson asked, softly tilting his head.

Damn, he was gorgeous. *Okay, Rebecca, get a hold of your libido.* "I'm fine, really."

Jackson smiled and little lines at the corners of his eyes fanned out, giving him a sexy air of mischief. "Sit down and talk to me for a while," he said as he sat and pulled out the chair beside him. "I haven't seen you in what? Ten years?"

Rebecca nodded and sat, thankful to be off her shaky legs.

"I'm really sorry about Josie," he said gently, compassion clear in his eyes.

"Me too." She smiled sadly. "I really didn't know her, Jackson. All these people knew her better than her own niece. I regret that."

Jackson shook his head. "These people didn't know Josie, Becca, any better than you did. That's the way Josie was, she liked her solitude."

Rebecca frowned and gestured toward a blue-haired woman sitting on the couch sobbing, clutching another woman's hand. "Mrs. Holt is devastated."

"Becca, Irene Holt never even met Josie. She attends any and all funerals and wails and carries on like that at every one of 'em." He narrowed his eyes and gave her a lopsided smile.

Rebecca's eyes widened and she tried not to laugh. "No way."

"Yep." Jackson grinned. "As for the rest of them, they're just being neighborly. Most of 'em still remember your family and you. You were pretty hard to forget with your 'pixie pest' ways. They're fond of you and wanted to be helpful, show they care."

"That's pretty incredible," she said, looking around at the quiet gathering. She looked back at Jackson, meeting his gaze. "What about you?"

"Oh yeah, they're fond of me too." He waggled his brows.

"Ha, ha." Rebecca narrowed her eyes.

Jackson's smile faded and his eyes darkened as he held her gaze. "I was always fond of you, Pixie. You were a great kid, even if you were a little pest that was constantly drooling over me and giving my girlfriends hell."

She had been such a little tomboy with wild young girl fantasies of being swept off her feet by the cutest boy in Jericho, or the whole wide world, for that matter. He'd called her his Pixie Pest and tugged at her long tangled hair and still made her young untried heart pound in her chest. Much like it was now. Only her heart wasn't untried anymore and she knew what that liquid pull low in her stomach meant.

"I'm not a kid anymore," she said without looking away.

Jackson's gaze traveled over her body. "I've noticed. I'm trying really hard to remember what a pain in the ass you used to be."

Rebecca lifted a brow. "I can still be a pain in the ass, Jackson."

"Hmm. I bet you can." He met her gaze again and held it. Her eyes dropped to his mouth. She wondered what those gorgeous lips would feel like on hers, on her breasts, on her stomach… For as long as she could remember she'd wanted Jackson to look at her like he was looking at her now. But he was making her feel way too hot, way too needy. She didn't need anyone. And after Todd Lawrence, the very last thing she needed was another relationship.

She stood. "I'm being rude sitting here. I better go mingle. Eat something." She needed to break the heavy silence that hung between them. He gave her a lopsided smile, took the plate and continued to watch her as he stood.

"Uh, there's iced tea in the kitchen, make yourself at home." She turned, took a deep breath and walked into the living room.

Time plodded along as Rebecca sat in the dim little living room with its floral prints and crocheted doilies. She listened and nodded and thanked those who stopped by. They asked about her parents and patted her hand sympathetically when she explained that her father had died three years ago of a heart attack. Their concern for her seemed genuine and the kind words and gentle touches were a surprising comfort to her. She found herself remembering her childhood and that rare country hospitality she'd missed for fifteen years.

It was late when the last person, none other than Mrs. Holt herself, hugged her, patted her cheek and left. Rebecca shut the door and leaned against it, shutting her eyes with a sigh. It warmed her heart that these people, regardless of their motives, not only spent time cooking for her, but also gave up their entire Saturday for her. It made her feel she'd been cheated.

"Everyone finally leave?" Jackson watched her with those observant silvery eyes of his.

He stood there with that lopsided smile and his hands in his pockets, looking like he'd just stepped out of GQ. Erotic images flooded her imagination and every cell in her body stood to attention. Endorphins flooded her system and sent that erotic heat washing over her body. Her cunt clenched, liquid arousal pooled between her sensitive lips, dampening her panties. Damn, it had been too long since she'd been touched.

"It appears so." She pushed away from the door. "Everyone except you."

Jackson watched her. Something in his eyes made her heart leap. She swallowed and gestured toward the dining room. "You should take some of that food home."

Jackson shook his head. "Already put up. There wasn't much left but it's in the freezer, labeled, dated and everything. Dishes are all washed and put up too."

"Wow." Rebecca smiled. Okay, he was looking way too perfect. "Thanks, Jackson."

"No problem. You're tired; you didn't need to have to face the mess." He stepped closer. "There's a plate for you in the fridge. Do I need to stay and make sure you eat it?"

She smiled up at him. If he stayed any longer she'd rape him for sure. "No, I'll eat it, I promise."

It annoyed her that she was disappointed that he wasn't going to try and take advantage of her. Her life was so up in the air. She knew she didn't need the entanglement but she wanted the warmth, the affection. She could feel the heat radiating from his body and she struggled not to lean into him.

"When are you going home?" His voice felt like a caress and she nearly whimpered.

"In the morning," she said breathlessly

"Are you selling the house?" he asked quietly.

She sighed and furrowed her brows. "I don't know yet. I had planned on it, but now…I don't know."

He watched her for a moment. "It was good to see you again, Pixie." He touched her face gently then took her into his arms. "Don't stay away so long next time."

She wrapped her arms around his back and resisted running them over the hard planes and over his round, tight ass. His body was hard and hot against hers. Her breasts felt heavy and swollen, her hardening nipples ached. She cringed knowing he could probably feel them pressing against his chest and pulled away, swallowing hard. "No, I won't."

He pressed his lips to her forehead then met her gaze. She watched in fascination as they darkened and turned stormy. She opened her mouth to say something and he lowered his head and kissed her mouth. A small kiss, lingering only seconds, but the impact was powerful. She looked up at him with wide eyes. He let her go and she felt suddenly cold.

"Be careful going home," he said hoarsely.

She nodded, folding her arms over her chest.

He turned and opened the door. "If you need anything let me know." He walked out onto the porch. "Lock up."

"I will." She fought her desire to ask him to stay.

"Goodnight, Becca," he murmured.

"Goodnight, Jackson." He pulled the door shut and she chained and bolted it. Rebecca walked into the spotless kitchen, her body humming with arousal. She ran her fingers through her hair in frustration. Sleep was definitely going to be hard to achieve tonight.

About the authors:

Lora Leigh is a 36-year-old wife and mother living in Kentucky. She dreams in bright, vivid images of the characters intent on taking over her writing life, and fights a constant battle to put them on the hard drive of her computer before they can disappear as fast as they appeared.

Lora's family, and her writing life co-exist, if not in harmony, in relative peace with each other. An understanding husband is the key to late nights with difficult scenes, and stubborn characters. His insights into human nature, and the workings of the male psyche provide her hours of laughter, and innumerable romantic ideas that she works tirelessly to put into effect.

As a young impassioned girl with a vivid imagination, Veronica Chadwick learned to express her thoughts, ideas and emotions through writing. As an adult she dabbled restlessly here and there with both poetry and prose. Finally, Veronica was introduced to Ellora's Cave and Erotica/Romantica. Her hot, rugged heroes and headstrong, vibrant heroines took control, helping her focus her energies and she knew without a doubt she had found her perfect niche.

In addition to writing, Veronica divides her time between home schooling her two gorgeous children, spending time with her wonderful husband who thankfully loves to cook and caring for their five cats and one very sweet beagle. Veronica has very eclectic tastes in just about every aspect of her life. Though she needs and cherishes all the quiet alone time she can manage to steal, she loves spending time with friends and chatting over a great cup of coffee.

Lora and Veronica welcomes mail from readers. You can write to her c/o Ellora's Cave Publishing at 1337 Commerce Drive, Suite 13, Stow OH 44224.

Also by Lora Leigh:

Bound Hearts 1: Surrender

Bound Hearts 2: Submission

Bound Hearts 3: Seduction

Bound Hearts 4: Wicked Intent

Bound Hearts 5: Sacrifice

Cowboy and the Captive

Dragon Prime

Elizabeth's Wolf

Feline Breeds 1: Tempting The Beast

Feline Breeds 2: The Man Within

Feline Breeds 3: Kiss of Heat

Law And Disorder 1: Moving Violations (with Veronica Chadwick)

Legacies 1: Shattered Legacy

Legacies 2: Shadowed Legacy

Men Of August 1: Marly's Choice

Men Of August 2: Sarah's Seduction

Men Of August 3: Heather's Gift

Men Of August 4: August Heat (12 Quickies of Christmas)

Ménage a Magick

Wolf Breeds 1: Wolfe's Hope

Wolf Breeds 2: Jacob's Faith

Wolf Breeds 3: Aiden's Charity

Also by Veronica Chadwick:

Educating Mr. Winters

Law and Disorder 1: Moving Violations

The Warlord's Gift

Why an electronic book?

We live in the Information Age—an exciting time in the history of human civilization in which technology rules supreme and continues to progress in leaps and bounds every minute of every hour of every day. For a multitude of reasons, more and more avid literary fans are opting to purchase e-books instead of paperbacks. The question to those not yet initiated to the world of electronic reading is simply: *why?*

1. *Price.* An electronic title at Ellora's Cave Publishing runs anywhere from 40-75% less than the cover price of the exact same title in paperback format. Why? Cold mathematics. It is less expensive to publish an e-book than it is to publish a paperback, so the savings are passed along to the consumer.
2. *Space.* Running out of room to house your paperback books? That is one worry you will never have with electronic novels. For a low one-time cost, you can purchase a handheld computer designed specifically for e-reading purposes. Many e-readers are larger than the average handheld, giving you plenty of screen room. Better yet, hundreds of titles can be stored within your new library—a single microchip. (Please note that Ellora's Cave does not endorse any specific brands. You can check our website at www.ellorascave.com for customer recommendations we make available to new consumers.)

3. *Mobility.* Because your new library now consists of only a microchip, your entire cache of books can be taken with you wherever you go.
4. *Personal preferences are accounted for.* Are the words you are currently reading too small? Too large? Too...**ANNOYING**? Paperback books cannot be modified according to personal preferences, but e-books can.
5. *Innovation.* The way you read a book is not the only advancement the Information Age has gifted the literary community with. There is also the factor of what you can read. Ellora's Cave Publishing will be introducing a new line of interactive titles that are available in e-book format only.
6. *Instant gratification.* Is it the middle of the night and all the bookstores are closed? Are you tired of waiting days—sometimes weeks—for online and offline bookstores to ship the novels you bought? Ellora's Cave Publishing sells instantaneous downloads 24 hours a day, 7 days a week, 365 days a year. Our e-book delivery system is 100% automated, meaning your order is filled as soon as you pay for it.

Those are a few of the top reasons why electronic novels are displacing paperbacks for many an avid reader. As always, Ellora's Cave Publishing welcomes your questions and comments. We invite you to email us at service@ellorascave.com or write to us directly at: 1337 Commerce Drive, Suite 13, Stow OH 44224.